The Opium Lady

Other fiction by JoAnne Soper-Cook

Waking the Messiah
The Wide World Dreaming
Waterborne

The Opium Lady

JOANNE SOPER-COOK

GOOSE LANE

Edited by Sabine Campbell.
Cover illustration courtesy of JoAnne Soper-Cook.
Cover and interior design by Julie Scriver.
Printed in Canada by Transcontinental.
10 9 8 7 6 5 4 3 2 1

National Library of Canada Cataloguing in Publication

Soper-Cook, JoAnne
The opium lady / JoAnne Soper-Cook.

ISBN 0-86492-370-8

I. Title.

PS8587.O72O65 2003   C813'.54   C2003-904738-5

Published with the financial support of the Canada Council
for the Arts, the Government of Canada through the Book Publishing Industry
Development Program, and the New Brunswick Culture
and Sports Secretariat.

The author gratefully acknowledges the support of the
Newfoundland and Labrador Arts Council.

Goose Lane Editions
469 King Street
Fredericton, New Brunswick
CANADA E3B 1E5
www.gooselane.com

To the memory of my grandmother,
Helena Fleming Trimm (1919-2003),
late of Kirkaldy, Fife, Scotland,
and New Chelsea, Newfoundland.

Contents

Acknowledgments

Ruth

HERE IS A PICTURE of Ruth: a 1940s woman standing in the shallow water of a summer pond, standing with another woman who might be a sister or perhaps a friend. The other woman has pulled her skirt up in a strange, self-conscious gesture, revealing her leg, which strides forward, independent of the rest of her. How very *avant garde* they are, with their summer clothing and their unabashed expressions, at least for that day and age. But this is a small town in southern Maryland, and Ruth is adopting an attitude of carefree insouciance in her striped sunsuit, with something clutched in her hand, something that might be a head scarf or a handkerchief or some portion of another woman's outfit. I can't be sure of colours, though, because the picture is black and white, and worse than that, it's faded now with age and crinkled round the edges. Ruth may be dressed in shocking pink with orange stripes, and I would never know. It's difficult to tell these things. It's difficult to reach into the past, and it's not as though she's someone in my own family — it would be easy, then, to construct some likely anecdotal evidence for her — but she's no one I have ever met. She is an old photograph found in a trunk, stashed in the upstairs bedroom (the smallest one, near the back of the house and overlooking the deserted baseball diamond). The only evidence, the only hint of provenance is the name, written in neat ballpoint script across the back of the picture: RUTH. In smaller letters, some later confidante has added, *Ruth in stripes with Mike's mother Alice.*

I like the look of her: she's slender and has a good figure, she's wearing that outrageous suit, which surely counts for something. If this is wartime, does Ruth work somehow for the war effort? I think she does. I think Ruth just got a job in a factory, making spare parts for bomber engines or putting together rifle shells, and is really proud of herself. In twenty years' time, her children will march off to Vietnam, and Ruth will go to the Wall in downtown Washington to trace their names hard upon her fleshy fingertips. But all of that is in the future. Ruth is frozen here in time, her feet and ankles swallowed up by water, wearing her outrageous suit, her shocking stripes. She looks far more poised than I am — me, driven here out of necessity, cast off like a faded winter coat and expected to drift somewhere along the wind and tides like the detritus of autumn leaves. *I have been shucked*, Ruth would say, *like an oyster.*

Her mother doesn't approve of her working and thinks that it's unseemly. In Momma's day, young ladies strolled about in tearooms wearing organdy dresses and sipping lemonade gracefully from frosted glasses, while the ceiling fans stirred the turgid Southern air. Momma thinks that Ruth should learn to dance Vienna waltzes, but Ruth will always be a swing kid, bopping blasphemously to Benny Goodman. Momma doesn't know that Ruth smokes cigarettes: purloined Chesterfields and Lucky Strikes and Players Navy Cut, out behind the factory on lunch break, crouching there amidst the stink of machinery and squandered time. Momma would have a fit. And Ruth has got herself a boyfriend, too, or that's what Momma thinks: LeRoy Hedge, son of a local grocer, thought to have good prospects, along with a perennial crop of pimples and a strangely woolly nose. LeRoy delivers groceries on his bicycle, pedalling miles every day to deposit shapeless bales of celery, wartime butter, tallowy and unreliable, and cans of precious milk. Ruth's momma refers to LeRoy always as HIM and HE, as though he were a member of the landed gentry, partaking of a mundane mortal life alongside ubiquitous tradesmen, Italians and Jews, the disenfranchised darky who runs the corner barbershop. Hagersfield is nothing but a small town, and LeRoy is very much the heir to all of it, since Mr. Hedge's Groceteria is typical of Yankee ingenuity. LeRoy wishes he were a Rebel instead but won't say such things to Daddy, who came here as a boy from somewhere up by Boston, who worked himself into the ground, who owns part of this town, goddammit.

But Ruth — her name really is Ruth-Ann — is from somewhere in the Midwest, some nebulous, untrustworthy place, some place that couldn't hold her parents, that could not hold or reclaim her. Momma always said you could tell who was trash by the state of her shoes, but Ruth-Ann (Momma *will* call her Ruth-Ann) has seen Tab Buffett's kids not wearing any, and she wonders what slot Momma might choose for kids like them. Momma was used to fancy ways, Ruth-Ann's daddy said, and it came from her being elected Harvest Queen in her Minnesota town. Daddy always said this darkly, glowering at Ruth-Ann from underneath his eyebrows, sitting at the kitchen table drinking soda from the can. He knew that Momma only married him because of his inheritance, what Momma called his "rightful share." Daddy was supposed to get everything

Granddaddy had and more, but he made a mess of the whole feed business and took to drinking secretly — sometimes aftershave lotion, if he could get it, because it smelled so much more pretty on his breath. Ruth-Ann thinks it isn't aftershave at all, she thinks it's that deodorant that Momma used to buy from Lois Greenlaw in the summertime, and in order to make it go further, Daddy cuts it with Royal Crown Cola. He also gets dressed every morning to go to work — he washes himself with great care, wets and combs his hair flat back on his head until it looks as though his skull is painted silver-grey. Ruth-Ann sees him do this every morning, sees him come out of the bathroom, all nicely dressed, and if his tie was caught a bit too tight around his neck, like a noose, and if his collar and cuffs were slightly frayed, no one (least of all Momma) had the indecency to mention it. Daddy'd been through a hard time lately — that's what Grandma always said — and a man needed to feel he had the respect of his family. It wasn't Ruth-Ann's place to mention the way her Daddy dressed, and if his breath smelled like underarms and Royal Crown Cola, she ought not to sass him. Nobody ought to sass her daddy. Nobody ought to sass the man, even if he told you that you were no good, even if he spent his time chasing other women at his work and having it off with them on sunny afternoons — nobody ought to sass a man for that. If you knew what was good, you'd keep yourself to yourself. Or else you'd run away: leave home and drift down South, rent yourself a house beside a deserted baseball diamond that no one ever plays on anymore, gaze out of your upstairs window while you rummage through a box of junk that some other family left behind. Leave everything behind and spend your time immersed up to your elbows in the scent of mouldered wood and fibreglass, burrowing through the attic of other people's secrets.

I think Ruth might work in a factory that makes helmets, army helmets that come rolling down the assembly line like great gleaming eggs, their green paint not yet hosed onto their shiny-smooth exteriors. They look like naked skulls, a multitude of empty craniums, waiting for the soul to get sprayed on. They have no thoughts inside them, no thoughts at all, and are content to wait as long as necessary for the touch that will complete them. They are held inside the factory walls, suspended there like leaden motes, steel receptacles. They feel they should wait for something, but they don't know what. Surely something will come along and recall their purpose to them or, if it is too intensely lost, invent some newer dictum. It takes an awful lot of energy to wait.

There's a black girl who works across the table from Ruth-Ann. Ruth-Ann has never spoken to her but sees her every day. Sometimes, when Ruth-Ann looks at her or happens casually to glance her way, the girl smiles shyly, as if they shared a secret of some kind, as if they knew something about the rows and rows of helmets sitting on the table, waiting to have their souls sprayed on them. Here is an example of the duplicity of women, the aberrant sisterhood that escapes like smoke between them; here is the manner in which a trusted friend, whether known or unknown, can corrode our lives. Never trust another woman, or you might end up in an abandoned house beside a baseball diamond, somewhere on the outskirts of a bedroom town in Maryland, waiting for some redemptive impetus to save you. Ruth-Ann sees the girl every day, sees her at lunchtime, sitting on a bench outside the factory, eating a sandwich in studious concentration and perhaps conscious discomfort. And as Ruth-Ann goes past her one sunny day, the girl says something. Ruth-Ann is wearing slacks to work, being *avant garde* again, and the girl upbraids her for it: "It's shameful, a woman in slacks." The other woman will always point out your differences, your failings and your shortcomings, even if with just a look; the other woman might be hard as nails, her face lacquered like Madame Tussaud, cheap and evil. You best mind what she says, don't sass her back. The other woman knows you. The next day Ruth-Ann shows up in a dress and penny loafers, and at lunch the black girl comments on her clothes: "Ain't no call for a woman to wear such shiny shoes." It becomes a sort of game, with rules that no one knows, rules that change and occupy a width of flux, impenetrable. Ruth goes home at night and scours all the closets in the house until Momma thinks she's taken with a bad spell, and Daddy goes to sit outside on the porch, so he won't have to hear the women fussing. It's no good for Ruth-Ann to accept a date with LeRoy Hedge, and when HE comes to call on HIS rickety bicycle, Ruth-Ann is nearly naked, shiftless, dressed only in her camisole and knickers. Momma puts her straightaway to bed. Ain't no call for a girl to carry on so, and LeRoy Hedge come to fetch her.

Here is Ruth, standing in the water, wanting desperately to make a surcease, to return again, to assume the mantle that she dropped, dashing heedless out of doors. Here is Ruth, waiting in her shameful clothes, waiting with her Lucky Strikes and Chesterfields.

Tobacco Road

I think her name is Millicent, the woman in this photo. She's standing with an older lady, perhaps some neighbour woman engaged to watch her for the day, and there is a line of laundry strung across the shack behind them. Millicent is smiling broadly, and she looks to be possessed of both ignorance and bliss in equal measure. I think she must have reached some sort of uneasy *détente* with herself. She has some disability, some weakness or lack in her, that excites an instinct of protection. She is the retarded half-sister of a group of girls that she has never met until this weekend, and even though they are not obligated, they have welcomed her into their tight circle as though she belonged there. Their father got a waitress pregnant — that's where Millicent came from — and he was a truck driver, hauling chickens to slaughter over the Tobacco Road, driving that long stretch of sometimes unpaved road from West Virginia to North Carolina. Tobacco Road, like every other road, leads away from Hagersfield.

Judy, Millie's mother, raised her daughter all alone, in a shack out by the railway tracks. She worked at a truck stop every day except Sunday, from seven in the morning until nine at night, and, since she had no kin in these parts, did for herself and her daughter whatever she could. During the day, Millie would be locked into her room with adequate food and water (for there was no murderous intent in Millie's mother, despite the high-piled disappointments of her life) as well as a bucket and some toilet paper, should she feel the urge. Because of this early isolation, Millie learned to meet her own bodily needs very well but never learned to talk, and this was a kind of hidden blessing, for if she couldn't talk, then she couldn't embarrass her mother's string of beaus and suitors that came sniffing round the shack in the summertime. She was essentially not there at all, except that she grew to be a tall, raw-boned girl with obstinately kinky hair that would never hold a style, and feet as large as cement blocks. Her eyes were dark and keen as raisins, with an expression that seemed to accurately fathom whatever secrets you were keeping. It was a well-known fact among the ill-educated folks that the simple-minded had something wild and fey about them, and it was no less so with Millie. Her mother might be entertaining a beau out back, and Millie would come sneaking round the corner and hover behind the door, listening to her mother as Judy giggled and preened.

But things go along, as things will, and in time Judy met a likely beau and decided well enough to marry him and brought Millicent to meet her long-lost sisters. Judy couldn't be expected to go to her new marriage carrying this hundred-weight of girl with her, and so it was agreed that Millie might visit with them, perhaps spend a week or two, and Judy would duly collect her after the nuptials were done. No one thought to question why this Judy had kept in contact with her former beau and the father of her large daughter — or perhaps they were too polite to ask. At any rate, the timing is perfect, since the girls' momma is visiting her sister in Charlottesville, where the sister just had a baby (not like Millie, one hopes) and will be gone for some time. Everything seems set for Millie to get to know her kin. Everyone should be glad. If Millie is being foisted off on these virtual strangers for the convenience of her mother, nobody bothers to mention it. It's the old-time code of hospitality and Southern politeness, and if you ain't kin yet, well, you might just be related somewhere back there, so come on in and put your feet up. This is the Southern equivalent of the stiff upper lip; it is an enforced politeness, dimly remembered from the motherland across the ocean. You could dump any wayward human specimen on these people, and they would take it in.

Judy gets out of the taxi with Millicent in tow — Millicent is eleven, but looks sixteen. She is tall and gangly with large hands and feet. Her hair is bobbed, and in some attempt at style, there is a pink ribbon tied around it. The sisters, standing patiently before their clean white house (which isn't the house in this picture — I don't know whose house that is), know instinctively that their father has somehow spawned this monster in secret in the dark; and that she has now been foisted upon them, and they will be obliged to care for her. With their mother gone, the girls don't quite know what to do. There are five of them all together, all of school age except Betty who is nineteen, and has a job as a stenographer (five days a week and half a day on Saturday) at a local lawyer's office.

"Y'all gotta take care of her." Judy is backing out the door even as she says this, neat in her shiny pink suit and dyed pink pumps that she will wear to be married in. "She's your sister, I reckon, and y'all gotta take her in."

Betty is the first and only of the sisters to speak. "We can't possibly — "

She is cut short by Judy. "Y'all *gotta*. I'm getting married to a shoe salesman over in Charlottesville. Y'all gotta take her. I cain't be responsible for no girl when I'm getting married in the morning." The slamming of the cab door is the end of it. The girls stand clustered on the front steps, watching Judy drive away and disappear in a cloud of dust. One of the younger girls starts to cry, but Betty shushes her, takes them all into the house.

Her mother is gone, and suddenly Millicent is alone amidst this crowd of strangers; since she does not speak, she cannot voice her anguish and so remains standing by the stove, gazing at them all, her giant moon face empty of emotion. If she believed in God, she would damn Him for abandoning her among these overweening girls, but she cannot grasp the concept of an almighty deity and so resigns herself to staring at them, moving slowly from one face to the next, her tongue caressing her bottom lip anxiously.

"What's wrong with that big girl?" Lucille, who is nine, clambers onto the kitchen table, so as to get a better look. "How come she's staring at us like that?"

Betty removes Lucille from the table, sets her on her feet. "She don't talk — she ain't never learned how." Betty knows this because she is her father's confidante and he has told her about his covert visits to Judy in the dead of night, or on his way back home from hauling chickens. He tells her things that he could never tell her mother. Betty feels no duplicity in this; on the contrary, she and Daddy are thick as thieves, and she's only doing him a favour.

"Where'd she come from?" Lucille is on her knees, gazing up under Millie's dress, which smells like piss and fabric softener; she is wondering if Millie is made the same as other girls but can't really tell because of Millie's thick-bottomed bloomers, made from an old bath towel.

"Our daddy made her with that woman." Betty gazes solemnly at them, each in turn, as though setting her own seal upon this knowledge. "And you ain't to tell *nobody* — you hear?"

The girls all sit around staring at Millie until Betty announces that it's time to be getting supper ready. She is always prepared for happenings like this and has half a roast chicken put by in the icebox and a potato salad that she made just that morning. Millicent eats quietly and with surprisingly good manners, and the girls are disappointed; they had hoped to see her dive into her plate face-first, cram handfuls of the potato salad into her mouth, belch and fart obligingly. After the meal is over and the girls are clearing the table, Millie does a curious thing: she goes to the corner of the big, sunny kitchen and lies down on the floor — lies down like a dog, her hands folded under her head.

Momma writes to say that she's going to stay a spell in Charlottesville with Aunt Regina, seeing as how Aunt Regina needs her just now. Reading between the lines, Betty understands the scope of the disaster: Momma knows about Millicent, knows the truth about Judy and their father and isn't ever coming home again. Betty's current beau, one Feston Dalyrimple, stops by one evening to take Betty out walking with him. When he sees Millie, he is aghast, and then laughs uproariously, wondering aloud where Betty found this thing. He circles Millie from all sides, feinting at her with his fists, as though gauging her reactions. "Where'd y'all git *her*?" he asks. "She some relative o' yourn?"

"She's a family friend," Betty tells him stiffly.

"Our daddy made her with some lady!" Lucille shrieks from around the corner, is slapped into silence by one of the other girls, who bear her away between them, kicking and screaming. Feston watches this in disbelief until Betty protests a terrible headache, ushers him outside and closes the door behind him. She wishes someone else were here to take charge of Millie, but Daddy is gone down Tobacco Road again, still hauling chickens, and Momma might be in Charlottesville forever. Betty decides that the best thing for all of them is if Millie appears to be a lodger, and so her sleeping quarters are relocated to the barn. This is a huge, ramshackle building situated on a patch of dirt that is whimsically referred to as the tater patch, though no taters have grown on it then or since. The barn was used to house the several sway-backed horses that Betty's daddy once owned, but now it was empty of all but hay and barn cats — evil, feral creatures fond of scratching and spitting. Millicent is fond of them, and feeds them tidbits of the meals that Betty brings her on a tray: cornmeal mush and hush puppies, sweet potato pie and grits.

And then some of the boys in town find out that Betty has a monster living in her barn and begin coming in droves after school to wander round the yard, hoping to catch a glimpse of this astonishing spectacle. They advance ideas as to what the monster might look like, creating gorgons and kraken in their minds. Betty tries in vain to drive them away, but they keep coming in ever-greater numbers. Lucille is excited by the great throngs and crowds of boys and passes her days playing cowboys and Indians with them, besting them at marbles and at trading cards, while Millie hides in the barn amidst a nest of cats. The boys and Lucille try in vain to entice her out, even coming to the barn door with small bribes or gifts of chocolate, a mutant frog with three hind legs. Millicent ignores them all, burrowing further into the nest of straw she has created for herself, hulking underneath last summer's hay.

And then Momma comes home from Charlottesville, riding on a mule of all things, like Christ on His Triumphal Entry. She rides into the yard, through the throng of school-boys, just as Betty is finishing the breakfast dishes. Momma is wearing trousers, a man's shirt, and a broad-brimmed hat to keep the sun away. Momma is her own woman, entirely independent of Daddy, strong and beautiful. Grandma Sykes says it's because Momma is of Irish stock, an ancient race of potato farmers who came over here many years ago, after Baltimore had first settled all the coast down here, and set up his small empire. Momma has long red hair and eyes as blue as the Irish Sea, and she doesn't put up with any guff from anybody, not even Daddy. She dismounts quickly, shooing all the boys away and calling them by name. "I knowed you was there, Jeb Sykes, and if you know what's good for you, you'll git down that road and keep right on goin'!" She swats them on the bottoms with her hat, chases them away. "I hope you girls been good while I was gone," she says, kissing each of them in turn. Betty cannot meet her mother's gaze, is terrified to look into her eyes.

They all turn as Millicent comes out of the barn (where she has concealed herself during the heat of the day). Her dress is dirty, smudged with the grime of old potatoes, and her hair is all awry. She is trailed by several of the barn cats, who cling to the hem of her skirt, who ride her shoulders like harpies.

"What's this?" Momma asks. "Is this some friend of yours, Lucille?" But even as she says it, she knows it cannot possibly be true — Lucille is only nine, and this gigantic girl has the solidity of a boulder.

"She belongs to Daddy." Betty can hardly force the sentence from her throat. For a long moment, the dusty yard and all around it is utterly silent and still, save for the anguished shrieking of a mockingbird, trapped nearby in an azalea bush. Momma looks at each of them in turn, can find no answer in their astonished faces.

"What do you mean, she *belongs* to Daddy?" But this is all that Momma says. She borrows a car from the maiden ladies down the road and, taking all the girls with her, drives to Raleigh. Millie makes the trip squeezed in between Betty and Lucille, still in her filthy dress, still with a barn cat on her lap. Momma stops in front of a diner and waits until she sees Daddy coming out, obviously liquored up and more pleased than he has need to be. Momma hisses at them all to stay just where they are but drags Millie from the back seat and, thrusting her at Daddy, tells him he's a no-good lying bastard, and that he ought to "take your trash back where it *come from!*"

Daddy watches Millicent with something like horror. He looks at all the girls, crushed into the car, gazing at him through the windows, wondering at the answers he might make.

"And tell me *where* have you been all this time?" People inside the diner come out to see what the commotion is; Momma is screaming so loud that people in the barbershop around the corner can hear every word she's saying. "What do you expect me to do with *her?*" She points at Millie, a jagged gesture full of hatred. Daddy and Millicent chance to speak to Momma at the very same moment.

"Tobacco Road," their daddy says.

Millicent replies, "Nothing." It is the first and only word that she will ever say.

Bertha and Her Daughters

Bertha is a housewife. She has four young daughters, all of whom depend on her, all of whom would be utterly bereft if Bertha managed to stand up one day and walk away from them . . . walk away, down the empty Southern road that leads towards the centre of Hagersfield, towards Hedge's Groceteria and the Indian Chief gasoline pumps, past Ettie Black's tiny scrimshaw post office with its broken signs and empty windows peering out at nothing, peering at the dust of a hot July morning. There are only three girls in this photo of Bertha, because the other girl is taking the picture, I'm sure of it. Bertha's husband left her just two days after her youngest girl was born, and that was seven years ago. He got up out of bed one morning, like he always did, sat there and laced up his shoes and put his hat upon his head and left. Just like that, with not so much as a by-your-leave. Maisie Hackett said she'd seen him in town the day before yesterday, but Bertha can't believe this. Bertha wouldn't want him back again, not after everything that passed between them, not after everything that has come and gone in seven years. She's made do on her own, like women will, and managed to keep body and soul together all this time. It's not for nothing that she was born a Zygant, of solid Norwegian peasant stock, expecting nothing and receiving less. Her face is always closed, stiff and resolute (in the photo she is smiling, but this isn't her usual expression), as though waiting for the buffeting of nightfall, which will ensure at least the disconsolate howling of the wind outside. She is a rock to these girls, the only thing they have, the only thing they want. The little one doesn't even know her daddy, and wouldn't like to know him if she did: he never drank except on Sunday afternoons when he would take a glass of beer out on the screen porch, and drink it slowly, measuring each sip as though it were the blood of life or his last breath. He smelled of turpentine and motor oil, smells that he could never wash from underneath his fingernails, no matter how hard the man scrubbed at the old pump out back in the yard. On Sunday mornings he would strip himself naked to the waist and stand out there, winter and summer, scrape his skin to redness with an ancient bath brush, worn to the nub of its bristles like a neglected tooth. Bertha would make herself turn away from the window, force herself not to watch him, and shush the girls away if they came near or tried to go outside. His torso was fish white, skin doughy-soft and hanging slack over the buckle of his belt, the loose flesh of his chest collapsing into hairy breasts, the nipples far too turgid and too red. He'd sluice himself all over with the icy water, snorting and blowing like a bull, scattering water from the loose edges of his lips, and Bertha would remind herself of how her daughters had come to her, what things were necessary to accomplish this, and she would shudder. She couldn't bear to let them watch their father bathing, not from any sense of modesty, but because it struck her that it was a disgusting spectacle, a sight that no decent young woman or girl ought to see. When he left, Bertha was glad. She'd put a little money by in a jelly jar, hidden in the cupboard underneath the kitchen sink; she would manage well enough if she were frugal, and Bertha had learned frugality as though it were a catechism.

She had learned it all those years ago, as a child in Norway, where she worked in a fish plant, side-by-side with her parents, both stolid and frugal people. For hours on end she would stand there, wearing rubber boots with heavy woollen socks inside, up to her ankles in cold, fishy water. The smell of fish guts sickened her, as she stood with rows of other people at a long metal table, filleting by hand: running the sharp blade of her knife up underneath the chin of a codfish, then yanking her hand back sharply, eviscerating it in one smooth stroke. By the time she was seventeen she could filet as fast as anyone else in the plant, had learned the art of standing there for hours, gutting innumerable codfish. And then Bertha and her parents and her brother Jens went on a ship to the United States, bypassing other avenues of emigration: Canada, England, and the cold and empty island of Newfoundland, crouched there on the periphery of the North Atlantic like a granite colossus. The trip itself was uneventful and took place in the spring: pushing through mountainous seas, the ship creeping past the great rearing heads of summer-seeking icebergs, until at last there were calmer waters, and the sea was no longer a cold green but a warm and reassuring blue. For long hours, Bertha would stand at the railing, braving the icy spray and the endless, scouring wind that buffeted her from all sides, and gaze out at the ocean, while streams and swirls of people drifted past her, each one isolated, each one wrapped against the cold. Their paths intersected with her own, their shadowed eyes chanced now and then to meet her gaze, but she kept herself aloof from them, cocooned inside her shabby winter coat, going below only to partake of meals with her parents and with Jens, who was seasick. Jens was weak in the chest, her mother said, and younger than Bertha, not as likely to survive a long sea voyage, especially in those days, after the war. He wasn't allowed to join Bertha on the deck and could only make a slow stroll about the ship whenever the weather was calm. Bertha wondered whether Jens was jealous of her relative freedom, but he didn't seem to mind. He lay below in his bunk, reading endless books and playing checkers with her father; slowly, imagining every move in advance, he docketed the progress of the game upon some score sheet in his head. He could adjust himself to the roll and sway of the ship, where Bertha couldn't. At night, while she lay awake in the bunk above him, Jens would sleep the sleep of the just, snoring with inimitable rhythm.

And then came the journey overland, from New York to Minnesota, where Bertha's father hoped to purchase land, to start again, to leave behind the cold stench of the fish sheds, the icy buffet of the ocean winds. Along the way, both children became ill with influenza, and by the time their train had pulled into the final station, Jens was gone. Bertha watched the porters carry his body off the train; it was draped in a railway blanket that covered up his face but left his lower legs and feet naked to the elements. She imagined it this way for years afterwards: Jens being borne away on a makeshift stretcher, one pale hand dangling over the side, the fingernails bitten to the quick and grimed with railway dust. One hand, rocking gently to the cadence of the porters' footsteps, as Bertha's mother sobbed into her handkerchief, devastated, inconsolable. At night, Bertha would lie in bed, drifting just upon the edge of sleep, and see that hand again, looming out of the darkness of her room, rocking gently as it made its way towards her, the fingernails grimed with dust and bitten down. She could remember the hand at will and recall its every feature to her mind, long after she had ceased to recollect what his face looked like, except that his watery blue eyes were forever rimmed with red, as though he were privy to some perpetual sorrow.

Bertha had a special friend in Margrete, the daughter of another immigrant, living side-by-side with Bertha's family in the wretched wooden shacks that their fathers had erected. No one had bothered to tell Bertha's father that a lifetime spent gutting codfish did not immediately qualify him for the job of builder. The house was rickety and strange, its interior walls tilting steadfastly toward the ground as though immeasurably weary. The windows fit awkwardly into the imperfect holes that Bertha's father had sawed, swearing under his breath and chewing the stump of his cigar between his teeth. The door was meant to keep the wind out, but it didn't keep the wind out, and late at night the prairie would come howling about the corners of the house.

Bertha and Margrete adventured far and wide together: camping, sleeping under the stars in summer when the prairie was hushed and still, the lambent stalks of grain nodding their weary heads beside slow-rippling brooks. They loved one another devotedly, and Bertha would always remark upon the pulse that beat under Margrete's skin, a mortal clock. One afternoon they were lying in a haystack, and Margrete was telling Bertha how she, Margrete, was growing breasts, how she had woken one morning to a terrible pain on each side of her chest, how she had cried out for her mother, who came to her and reassured her that it was natural. "They hurt me every morning," Margrete said, "and at night, when I go to bed, it pains like needles in my chest." At the time of this revelation, Bertha was still flat, still straight and boyish, and she held her mouth against the pulse under Margrete's left breast, embracing it like a holy thing, an oracle. She and Margrete pressed their palms together and promised, *swore,* to be friends forever . . . but there was something sinister in the Minnesota sky, something ominous in the hard, nacreous blue. For a moment, she glimpsed it again, the hand of her brother Jens, coming closer, taking substance from the shadows, but when she opened her eyes, it was gone, and only the hard blue sky above them. In years to come, she will remember this moment, just as she can easily recall the hand.

One night at supper, Bertha's father tells the family that he has lost everything — he is bankrupt. Bertha wonders at the shape of this word, *bankrupt,* and the way it felt strange and foreign on her palate. Her mother keeps on eating, as though nothing were going on, then stands and clears the dishes, brings them to the kitchen. Bertha feels her eyes grow, wider and wider, as her father tells her that Lars Van der Hooeven wants to marry her — Lars, who is a wealthy man, who owns a fleet of broken-down vehicles, that he works on by himself. Bertha's father says this and wipes the food out of his moustache. Bertha is horrified. She has seen Lars once or twice, but on Sunday he comes for dinner. He is big and red-haired, with a coarse red complexion like salted leather, and vacant blue eyes. He eats quickly, grunting whenever he is spoken to, unless he is discoursing freely on the state of his vehicles, the rusted cars and trucks and school buses that dot the landscape behind his house. If Bertha's father asks about Lars's school bus, he becomes radiant, excited, talks as though his machines were women to him, a harem to do his bidding. His big red hands grip the cutlery, and his blue eyes are illuminated as they never are at other times. His thick red fingers caress the tabletop, and he shifts himself in his chair, rotating his hips as though screwing himself down more firmly into the cushions. For Bertha he is repugnant: a *disjecta membra* of unrelated parts carelessly shackled together, a Frankenstein monster. She knows she will be made to marry him. She knows this is her duty: to save her family at the expense of herself.

On their wedding night, Lars is insatiable and rapes Bertha, tearing off the wedding dress that her mother made, sewing for many laborious hours, down to the embroidered roses attached about the hem. No one has told Bertha what to expect, and she is shocked. Her mother had called her into the sitting room the day before; she had hugged her, kissed her dryly on both cheeks and told her always to obey her husband. No one told her what would happen. No one told her that conjugal piety led to distress. Lars mounts her imperiously, pressing down on her, forcing his swollen phallus into the space between her legs, rutting into her savagely. In the morning, Bertha is mortified to see blood all over the sheets, here is Lars lying in this bed in her mother's house, with her parents asleep in the next bedroom. Are they impervious to the horrors taking place behind the door? Lars takes Bertha again and again and finally collapses into sleep or something like insensibility, while Bertha lies awake, dry-eyed in the dark. That night, she again dreams of Jens and his ragged hand.

Soon Bertha finds herself pregnant, and in short order there are four daughters, all lovely, but very much demanding their share of her time. Somewhere in amongst the detritus of the years, Lars sells his junkyard in Minnesota, moves the family down to Maryland, establishes a dumping ground there, selling parts and scraps. Bertha lives with Lars on this great, sprawling junkyard that is their home, but then his business begins to fail, and he becomes angrier. He is always angry now, always demanding that Bertha drop whatever she is doing and tend to his needs. At night, he sits at the dining-room table and pores over the many receipts that he keeps stuffed in a shoebox underneath their bed. He will not tell her what is bothering him, and Bertha does not dare to ask. She is afraid of him, as she has always been, only now she is more afraid of him than ever. She thinks he might kill her, and she imagines ways that she might defend herself. He takes to drinking more: no longer is one beer on Sunday sufficient, now there are empty whisky bottles, empty vodka bottles teetering precariously behind the front porch door.

He returns home drunk one night, comes barrelling through the door, crashing into the house, trying to knock down obstacles with his head. For the first time in many years, the nights are cold, and Bertha dreams more and more now of her home in Norway, of icy winters in the freezing icy water, cutting icy codfish with her knife. A freak storm has blown up from the gulf, is tracking its way along the coast to Hagersfield, taking out power lines and laying a thin film of grainy snow on all the roads. Old Man Hedge the grocer is outdoors, trying to reach another town on skis; he is struck and killed by a train as he is attempting to cross the tracks. Cars lie stranded in ditches; someone froze to death on the road coming into Hagersfield, someone without a proper winter coat.

Bertha has put the girls to bed and is chopping up chickens to make soup. She hears Lars come in but does not turn to greet him, accustomed as she is to his sudden rages, his disregard for all rights of property or space. He wraps his thick red hands around her waist, but she pushes him away, refuses him for the first time in their married life. The wind has begun to howl outside the door, and Lars begins to shout and Bertha lays the dismembered chickens in the sink, turns and brings the cleaver down upon his hand. She severs all four fingers, watches without emotion as they fall into the sink and rest there, unmoving, their grimy nails showing black against the chickens' snowy flesh. She thinks about those fingers and their heinous activity, digging in her flesh all these years to gain a better hold. She watches as Lars flings open the door and flees into the night, leaving Bertha with his cut-off fingers. The children come out to the kitchen to see what's going on; Bertha hides their father's fingers in the pocket of her apron and comforts the children, sends them back to bed. The fingers press heat into her belly, and she goes quickly through to the back yard, digging furiously in the ice and snow, chopping through the surface with her cleaver. She buries them in the dark, then goes to bed and falls asleep, dreaming, not of her brother's hand and not of her husband's severed fingers, but of a clean expanse of snow, white and resolute.

This is how Bertha's husband left her: not in the hazy heat of a summer morning, not deliberately, but quickly, driven out into the darkness like a fleeing troll. Bertha cannot tell her daughters such a story, and so she invented the tale of how their father walked away one morning, got up out of bed and laced his shoes, settled his hat upon his head and moved out into the dusty road. The younger girls cannot know the truth, but Bertha's eldest daughter does, and sometimes, in the night, she dreams ugly scenes about the chickens and sees her father's severed fingers floating to her in the darkness, their nails black and bitten to the quick.

Six months later the train comes, bringing Margrete, who never married. She immediately carries Lars's clothes to the trash and drops them in.

Life Lessons

Violet looks like she might be a schoolteacher, fresh out of a very progressive women's college, somewhere like Vassar or Brown. But Violet has a certain timidity of soul and very "modern" ideas about education that do not sit well with others around her. The year is 1919, on the very threshold of the Jazz Age, that wasteland of money and excess and violent American dreams. Violet had this picture taken as a gift for someone: she doesn't look old enough to have graduated from some college, but she did, and here she is. She has the look of an intelligent woman, but a woman who nevertheless does not hope for much. Perhaps she has already been disappointed in love, but there's no way to tell from this old photograph. Her arms are thick and sturdy, and the simple skirt and blouse she's wearing disavow any notion of sexiness. She pretends not to want any part of that, but her eyes are lively, and they hint at secrets left unspoken. Perhaps she lives a rich inner life; perhaps she understands exactly how lucky she is. She knows how sparse opportunities are and how lucky she is to have received a decent education. She knows the value of being grateful and practises this gratefulness daily, never allowing herself to pine after or even think about those other parts of life that she has never tasted. She will discipline herself in this — she will pretend to be easily satisfied. She will act as though everything she has is just enough, that more would be surfeit and wasteful. Some women are very good at that sort of thing and train themselves from very early in their lives to accept the little that is offered, to arrange their choices on a plate and pick amongst them with a deliberate lack of appetite. What else could she do? How else can a woman like Violet conduct herself? Our mothers always told us, *Don't be greedy! Save some for someone else!* And we have heeded this advice. We have heeded it to our detriment.

Violet is lucky enough to be present at an afternoon reception for the Archbishop of Washington and some other frightfully imposing people. It doesn't matter how she got there, merely that she is — at the house of a friend's parents. Perhaps this friend was Violet's roommate in college: they shared a room and exchanged such confidences as are thought proper in the context — talk about boyfriends and dresses and the value of earning one's own money, and whether all those other people were suffering overmuch now that the Great War had finally ended. If Violet had any hidden, arcane yearnings, she would have kept them to herself, unable to trust this friend. We are always unable to trust the other woman, no matter what sorts of masks she wears. Violet is very good at pretending, assimilating to make herself agreeable; she would have traded giggly secrets about the inevitably tweedy young men that one meets at college, and vowed never to let a boy go "too far" until she was safely married. This would have been expected, and Violet absolutely gave it, and this is why everyone likes Violet, why she has so many confidantes and intimate girlfriends. She is so very agreeable, as plain girls often are. She has learned to expect nothing because she receives nothing.

But here is Violet now at the afternoon reception at the house of this faceless friend from college, and the Archbishop of Washington is there, looking in his flowing robes like some sort of kaleidoscopic sunset. He is a fat old man with a red nose like Santa Claus, the result of too much drink. There might be something in the punch, or perhaps he is tippling secretly from a bottle of his own. At this moment, he is talking to Violet's college friend — perhaps her name is Mary Ann — and regaling her with stories that are perhaps a little bit off-colour, for a cleric. Mary Ann is pretty in a flashy sort of way, but she is not someone who will ever settle down to the kind of useful life that Violet might expect. Indeed, Mary Ann has entered into a secret engagement with a boy from Princeton, without her parents' knowledge or consent. The only reason Mary Ann went to college in the first place was so that she could find a husband — to get her M.R.S. Degree, as people say. Mary Ann's parents are moderately wealthy, though her father's fortune is of rather shadowy origins, and some say that he might have been supplying Johnny Turk with drugs during the Great War, although no one has ever been able to prove this. It's not a big deal in any case, for Violet knows of dozens of men, young and old, around Hagersfield where she comes from, who engage in all manner of under-the-table activities in order to turn a profit. Unlike Violet, Mary Ann expects everything.

At this afternoon reception with the corpulent archbishop, Violet learns by eavesdropping that there is a job opening at St. Margaret's, a prestigious girls' school in Washington, D.C. She overhears this from the archbishop himself, as he stands ladling dark liquid from the punch bowl, his puffed red face gleaming with sweat. "And I know for a fact that they can't find anyone even remotely qualified — especially not now, with everything in such upheaval." He pauses, mops his sweating brow with a handkerchief the approximate size of a tablecloth. "Where we'll find someone, I don't know."

This is Violet's cue, she approaches him, clutching her courage in both hands. She is dressed in a simple white dress, and her hairstyle is severe and plain, entirely unadorned with clips or ribbons. She catches him alone at the punch bowl, where he is filling glass after glass, greatly enjoying himself. He smells bad: like overripe, yeasty flesh, like underpants or dirty teeth. "Hello, my dear girl!" The archbishop pours Violet a cup and she realizes that someone has spiked it — she has promised her parents that she would never consume alcohol, now a mouthful of it has already passed her lips, is sliding down her throat too fast to be reclaimed. The archbishop is regarding her oddly, and Violet decides that the best thing for her to do is to drink it — simply drink it, and imagine that it gives her the ability to be as frank and charming as Mary Ann is.

"I want the job." She cannot bring herself to tell him how she gained this knowledge, and indeed, he does not ask. He is more concerned with examining the outline of her body underneath her nondescript white dress, the turn of her slender ankles. He is celibate, he tells his friends and intimates, but not dead, and wasn't Our Blessed Mother also a woman? "The teaching job, at St. Margaret's. You see, I've just graduated from teacher's college, and I'm certain I could fill this position." After this speech is done, Violet is amazed that she has even said it — amazed that she could find the necessary fortitude to summon such a speech.

"Do you?" the archbishop fills her glass again, unbidden.

"Well, come by on Monday. I'm sure we can have a look at your credentials."

Violet is an inveterate eavesdropper, a listener at doors; all her life she has been doing this; and perhaps it's curiosity that drives her, but also a desire to order her own universe. She listens to conversations at parties and dances, and she listens at various doors and in stairwells. She listens on sidewalks and while waiting at the library, and she listens in waiting rooms and hospitals. She knows more about you than you could ever know about her because you have not her skill of listening.

"I heard you got an interview!" Mary Ann is suddenly by her side, bubbling and snapping, shimmying from the inside out. "I'm so thrilled!" She is talking to Violet, but her eyes are wandering around the room, stopping finally on a flaxen-haired young man with protruding upper teeth, who is making visual overtures in her direction. When Violet goes into the kitchen to get a glass of water, she overhears the young man talking about Mary Ann.

"She's so easy . . . you know she's easy . . . you want to rent a room with Mary Ann, just say the word!" They break off into easy laughter, and even though Violet can't see them, she knows they are elbowing each other, offering each other knowing glances. "She's better than that friend of hers — what's her name? Violet?"

Violet leans closer to the kitchen door, her ear pressed against the wood; she is just in time to hear, ". . . vinegar-faced old maid!" and understands the cost of listening at doors. She wants to warn Mary Ann about the young men — about all young men — but when she goes back into the living room, Mary Ann is talking familiarly to them in the corner and Violet is forgotten.

On Monday, Violet goes to St. Margaret's, fear hammering

in her breast like a wild animal. She has seen enough of the archbishop to know that he was drunk that night, and her common sense warns her that he might not even recognize her, that the nuns at St. Margaret's might not have ever heard of her. How to cover an embarrassment like that? But the drunken old cleric has kept his promise, and she is met by Sister Ignatia who is about Violet's own age, with thick spectacles like the bottoms of jelly jars. A quick examination of Violet's college grades, and Sister Ignatia announces that Violet can have the job and will start tomorrow. "We expect a high standard from our teaching staff," Sister Ignatia says, standing to signal that the interview is over. "A high standard."

Violet reaches to shake her hand as Sister Ignatia attempts to smile. On the way out, Violet sees a tall, thin, dark-eyed girl with long, dark hair gazing at her with a familiarity that is unsettling. Violet has almost moved to greet her when she realizes that the girl is a stranger, no one she knows. And yet the girl resembles Violet, when Violet was a young girl: there is the same expression in the features, the same disconcerting candour in the gaze, the same attitude of the body that says *I expect nothing from life.*

The new job becomes her, and Violet settles in well. The dark-eyed girl is in her class; she never speaks, but listens with a kind of burning intensity as Violet outlines the lessons on the blackboard. Sometimes Violet chances to meet her gaze, and something in it frightens her; it seems to peer deep into her soul, uncovering all her secrets, and she shrinks from it and from the girl whose presence seems suddenly to expand until it is filling the entire room.

Violet learns from her parents that Mary Ann is getting married; she and her new husband will be setting up house in Pennsylvania. This is not shocking: it is no more than Violet has expected all these years, and Mary Ann is eminently suited to be a wife, just as she, Violet, is not. Violet is happy for her, and tells Mary Ann as much as they sip coffee together at a lunchroom near St. Margaret's School. "He sounds absolutely wonderful," Violet says, with something of the old self-effacing good humour that carried her through her college years. "And I know you'll be very happy. Where are you registered? Or have you got your china and silver already set aside?"

Mary Ann's face quivers as Violet says this, as if the skin were sliding off the bones; she reaches across the table and captures Violet's hand: "I'm going to have a baby."

"Of course you are — many babies, I dare say — "

"In about eight months. I'm going to have a baby." She tries to appear sober and matronly, but bursts into a fit of hysterical giggling, upsetting two businessmen deep in conversation at the next table. "Oh, it's true! It's all Donny's fault, too. He said I wouldn't get in trouble if we kept our shoes on. And I believed him!" She covers her mouth with her hands and shrieks with laughter; the two businessmen get up abruptly and leave.

"Donny *who*?" Violet can't place him.

"Donny — at the party. Remember? With the Archbishop." She simpers, sipping her coffee. "Oh, we knew each other before that. Sissie introduced us, at her sister's coming-out party. It's love, sure as shooting."

Now Violet really feels sorry for Mary Ann. She knows that Mary Ann will marry Donny, have this baby, and perhaps more babies after that, and that she, Violet, will continue to teach, this vocation of hers stretching onward, into infinity. There is something destined about it, something inescapable.

Mary Ann will awaken at thirty-five or forty to discover that Donny is seeing other women, or that her children are dull and unintelligent, and she will wonder why. She will wonder why she allowed herself to be so blindly led.

The dark-eyed girl at school is somehow disturbing to Violet, for reasons that she cannot readily identify or understand. It seems like she is waiting for something: that she wants something from Violet that Violet cannot give. Time and again Violet sees the girl at the edge of her vision and turns just as the girl vanishes as quickly as a puff of smoke. When Violet calls on her in class, the girl replies politely, but there is something careless and empty in her self-assured gaze, something that chills Violet to the marrow of her soul. Her manner of speaking, the way she carries herself, these remind Violet of Mary Ann, and she feels very afraid for the girl and for herself.

Violet questions Sister Ignatia about it: "There's a particular girl in my class — very pretty girl, dark eyes, long dark hair —"

"Oh, you must mean Janice," the nun (whose name is really Julia) replies. She is pouring tea for herself and Violet in the tidy confines of her room at St. Margaret's, offering a plate of tiny cakes and shortbread cookies. Behind her glasses, Julia's eyes are a clear and startling green, like newborn grass, and her skin is dewy and smooth, the skin of a young girl. She and Violet are the same age, but Violet feels monumentally older, as if she has seen and done so much more than Julia. She wonders what sort of life Julia has led, before the convent, before St. Margaret's, but she does not dare to ask. Her old habit of listening at doors has turned up nothing. Julia is an enigma, just as the dark-eyed girl is an enigma, and Violet can penetrate neither of these mysteries, but must remain outside, gazing at what is essentially a social mantle, donned for the benefit of the public gaze.

"Have you always been a nun?" This question slips past her usual reserve, and she is momentarily embarrassed until Julia smiles gently, a smile with great personal forbearance in it.

"Goodness, no!" She takes the teapot to her little table, turns on the hotplate under the kettle in anticipation of a fresh pot. "I did have a childhood, Violet — a mother and a father, two brothers."

"I'm sorry," Violet mumbles this into her teacup. "I shouldn't pry."

"I entered the convent when I was seventeen — even then, I knew that a cloistered life was what I wanted." Julia leans down to gaze at Violet, smiling impishly. "It isn't a death sentence, Violet. I am free to leave any time I wish. But I don't wish to. St. Margaret's is my home."

Violet feels as though she has blundered into an area she has no business in. She wants to make Julia stop talking, turn the conversation back to the dark-eyed Janice and her vitriolic look.

"Besides which, my marriage to Christ is as real as marriages get, Violet." Julia fills the teapot, her small hands quick and certain. "He has come to me. We have consummated our union." Julia straightens her back and wonders if she has said too much. Violet, who has only a vague notion of faith, is amazed.

"But you were asking about Janice." Julia brings the teapot to the table, freshens both their cups. "I must tell you, since I've been here at St. Margaret's, I've met many strange and prickly girls . . ." The anecdote wanders, is lost in silence for a moment. Julia tells Violet that Janice is an orphan, a ward of the Church, and will probably be fostered into the convent at St. Margaret's as soon as her schooling is done. Janice lives at St. Margaret's year-round and spends the Christmas holidays with the nuns. She speaks only when necessary, Julia says, and then in monosyllables: Janice's mother ran off with a card sharp, and her father shot himself while Janice was at school. This seems to Violet a strangely pithy story, one without a proper ending. She feels sorry for Janice and wonders if she ought to do something for her, enact some little kindness that might be remembered. She sees her younger self in Janice, the shocking recognition of her own frustrated anger, her helplessness. She wants to show Janice how anger might be parlayed into something different. She wants to confer the life lessons that she herself has earned.

She begins to leave small treats in the girl's school desk: an apple, some candy, a purple pencil, an eraser in the shape of a cat. She watches Janice carefully for any sign of acknowledgment, but there is none. The gifts become more extravagant: a leather pencil box, a circle pin, a silver bracelet. Violet contrives to be present as Janice discovers these items, hoping for some recognition which never comes.

She is grading papers at her desk one day, and there are hesitating footsteps. When she moves to speak, Janice turns and runs away, the heels of her shoes flashing in the dusted light of early afternoon. Violet wonders if the girl has vanished, but after lunch Janice is there in her usual place, staring at Violet with malevolent eyes.

There are no more gifts.

Dolly Friday

Here is Dolly Friday: a minister's daughter, a very pretty and spirited girl who has dozens of beaus. In this photograph, she is standing with two brash young swains who seem more interested in the camera than in her. Her skirt is plain grey flannel, and, like all ladies of her generation, she is wearing a modest cotton blouse, buttoned to the neck. Her hair is blonde and curly, her lips are red, and she has the kind of Saxon beauty that any man would fall for. She seems happy with herself, and I can't help wondering why, since the men in this picture don't seem to be paying much attention to her. Perhaps she is the sort of girl who doesn't require the kind of masculine approval that is necessary to the rest of us; if some man threw her over or even threw her out, she would dust off her flannel skirt and adjust her demure cotton blouse and hurry on her way, perhaps with a run in her stocking, but otherwise unaffected. I wonder how women manage such feats, and what is the secret of their untouchability? To go through life relying only on yourself is, I think, a feat worthy of admiration, or at the very least, a quiet approval. These women shine out in the dullness of my imagination like scattered beams of light, as indicators of womanhood in its truest form. I wish I could be independent, as they are. I wish I had the presence of mind, or the strength of thought to conduct myself always in a manner befitting a woman on her own. That's what I am now — or at least, that's what all the magazine articles tell me: a woman alone, a woman at odds with the world, a woman without the cozy buffer of a man by her side. Whatever choices I make now, I make them entirely for myself. It's been that way ever since I came here, moving south from my island home, ringed about with the cruel tides of the Atlantic. I've been alone for months now, ever since he uttered that most weighty of pronouncements, *I don't love you anymore*, and ushered me out into a world as cold as I am.

But here is Dolly Friday, going to Chicago on the bus to visit her father's sister, an aunt also named Dolly, as though it were some sort of family tradition, something handed down like odd bits of silverware and lacy tablecloths. Aunt Dolly is a spin-ster who lives alone and paints village scenes upon stretched canvas, after the manner of John Constable: lusty farm lads hefting bales of hay onto a laden cart while large-breasted milkmaids bare their common ankles and their shoulders. Aunt Dolly is a kind of Virginia Woolf, a woman on her own, a woman who has rejected the familial appellation and calls herself "Auntie Dee" because it has a vaguely English ring to it. Of course, the rest of Dolly's Episcopal family regard Auntie Dee as merely eccentric, but not dangerous — not dangerous, say, in the way unmarried working women are, or those who take lodgings together in the ubiquitous Boston marriages favoured by the Yankees. Auntie Dee had a woman friend once — many years ago — who died in an untimely fall from a ladder, and since then, she has preferred her own company, exclusive of all others. Dolly secretly admires this in her and rejoices that her family has seen fit to let her go and visit this paragon of womanhood in faraway Chicago.

Dolly announces the anticipated trip at supper, while she and her parents (there are no other siblings, Reverend and Mrs. Friday having not had either the will or the inclination to repeat the progenitory process) are eating breast of chicken with the last of the summer mushrooms. The Reverend will not allow these cuts to be named as they are; for the purposes of familial harmony he insists they be referred to only as 'torsos' and wife and daughter happily agree to this. Besides the chicken torsos, there are fine red-skinned potatoes, roasted to a golden sheen, and little onions, as well as a formidable salad. Reverend Friday's congregation is sizeable, and he considers himself lucky to escape the poverty that seems to dog some others of his profession, especially the Baptists, who deserve whatever they get. It is for this reason that Reverend Friday chose the seminary all those years ago: that he might get a decent living for his family and himself, in an established church — and not have to wash the feet of the filthy poor, as the Baptists did in white-trash towns like Possum Trot. He likes to think that he is from the South but not *of* the South — that is to say, he is refined in his manners and speech, and does not pick his teeth at table or whistle various old drinking songs while shaving in the morning.

After supper is over, and the chicken torsos adequately dispatched into the digestive systems of the collective Fridays, Dolly goes upstairs to choose the outfit she will wear on the bus. She lays out a selection of dresses, hats and shoes, all of the same variety as she is wearing in the photograph, all eminently suitable for the daughter of a minister of religion. When she hears her mother's footsteps on the stairs she knows, even before her mother lays a hand upon the doorknob, that she will be subjected to one of Mama's talks. When Dolly turned thirteen, Mama came to her room especially to give her a talk — about how girls grew up to behave like respectable young ladies, and didn't chew gum, giggle in church, or speak to young gentlemen unless spoken to first. At the end of the talk, Mrs. Friday left a package of Kotex pads on Dolly's bedside table and went away, her head bowed like a reluctant penitent who has finally done her duty.

"Your father and I feel" — Mrs. Friday's talks are always prefaced with this statement, as though she were connected to the Reverend Friday by some invisible cord, always subject to whatever tugging he might choose to make — "that you ought to be told about Auntie Dee before going to Chicago." Mrs. Friday sits on the end of Dolly's bed, unsure whether to stay or go, and takes to twisting her wedding rings around and around on her finger, so that her diamonds catch the available light and throw it out upon the walls in dazzling sparks and wheels of colour. Dolly is so caught up in this kaleidoscope that she hears her mother's talk in variegated bits and pieces; clearly, Auntie Dee is different in some way that is abhorrent to the Reverend and Mrs. Friday, but Dolly cannot clearly understand *how*.

"Dolly, are you listening?" Mrs. Friday sits forward, her shoulders rounded in anticipation, her eyes glistening behind her spectacles.

The truth, of course, is that Dolly has been so enraptured with the impromptu show of light and colour that she hasn't grasped a word, but to spare her mother's feelings, she says, "Yes, of course. I understand." She does not understand that what her mother has revealed is entirely beyond her comprehen-sion. It all passes in a blur; Dolly is eager to get on the bus, to see Auntie Dee in Chicago, to glimpse something of life outside the rectory. She imagines that there are many sorts of adventures waiting to happen to her, and she is eager for every one of them. Perhaps she might fall in love, she thinks, and be swept away by a handsome stranger. These are the sorts of dreams that Dolly keeps locked inside her heart. They are the eternal dreams of women and girls who yearn to be the con-quest and not the conqueror, as though the former claimed some obscure status that is naturally denied the latter.

On the appointed day, her parents take her to the bus station, handling her luggage carefully, as though the bags were filled with Tiffany or Fabergé instead of Dolly's schoolgirl skirts and sweaters. Dolly is enormously excited about every aspect of the journey, and she kisses her parents absentmindedly, anxious to get aboard the bus and begin her great odyssey.

She is intrigued to see the landscape sliding past her window, and she is impressed at the way the driver announces all the stops into a microphone. And she is thinking about Auntie Dee, recalling photographs of her, and wondering what Auntie Dee will think of her, now that she is all grown up.

While she is there dreaming her young woman's dreams, a man seats himself beside her, uninvited, and Dolly looks up suddenly, looks up into his face and offers him a flustered greeting. Perhaps the done thing is to seat yourself with strangers, she thinks, or perhaps there aren't enough seats for everyone. He is older than she is and much more sure of himself, and he picks his teeth lazily (although he has eaten nothing that she can see) and says, "Yer jest a li'l slip of a thing, aren't you."

His name is Roy Farber, he says, and he's a Bible salesman from Virginia. He sells Bibles to hotels and motels, and "that's why there's a Bible on every night table. Didn't know that, didya?"

A woman of more wit and experience would immediately have dismissed him as a masher, but Dolly is an innocent; she is impressed with his tales of travel, of hobos he has encountered on the rails, of rich ladies who have taken him in as a long-lost son. He tells her about the big hotels he's been in, in places like New York City, and this must have some sort of elusive savour, for he repeats it several times like a pleasant taste inside his mouth. "You ever ben in a hotel, li'l girl?"

"My father thinks hotels are immoral," Dolly tells him, and finds it exciting that he guffaws loudly at this, slapping his knees. Something dark and wild rises in her; she wants him to spirit her away, take her to New York City, set her up as a fancy lady in a fancy apartment on Fifth Avenue. He hints that he has many business connections and can do this, if it's what she really wants. He says this several times as well, and it clearly has the same sort of savour for him. By the time they reach Chicago, Dolly agrees to accompany him to see the great hotels he has told her about. Part of her remembers the old, dusty stories she's been told and things hinted at by her mother, but Dolly doesn't care. She wants this (or thinks she does) because she has no real idea what "this" entails. She does not know the truth outside the relative safety of the bus, nor the dark valleys from which men like him are spawned. She doesn't know, and so she goes with him — to a hotel room, where he registers them as Mr. and Mrs. Roy Farber, signing with a flourish. Dolly has never been in a hotel and cannot grasp the significance of the bellhop's knowing smirk as he unlocks the door and pockets the tip. Roy Farber opens his suitcase, which is filled to its very rim with Bibles, and loosens his collar. He has produced an evil-smelling cigar from somewhere and is smoking it, and then his arms are around her, his breath blowing hard against her skin. "You know what you came here for," he whispers, grasping her around the waist, crushing her ribs underneath his hands. "You know you want to get dirty with me." His mouth is on hers, smothering her, and his hands slide up underneath her skirt, pawing at her buttocks, leaving bruises. "Let old Roy show you how it's done —"

But he gets no farther than this, for Dolly, suddenly in possession of her senses, emits a piercing scream that brings the bellhop, the chambermaid and the hotel detective, in that order; they burst into the room to confront Roy Farber, who by this time has removed his trousers and is standing near the chest of drawers clad only in his underpants. The bellhop subdues him while the detective cuffs him, and Roy is led screaming down a back stairwell, without his trousers. Dolly can't think what else to do, and so she sits down on the bed, her nostrils full of the scent of Roy's cigar, her fingers trembling. "Take me away from here," she whispers once, then louder and louder again, until she is screaming: "Take me away from here, *oh* take me away from here!"

She is put into a taxi and sent to Auntie Dee's, who isn't nearly as strange as she had thought, but rather a kind of homely maiden aunt. She tells Auntie Dee everything about Roy Farber, about his oily hair and his great big hands and the suitcase full of Bibles that he was sent to sell, as though on a holy mission. "He put his hands on me!" she wails, but Auntie Dee is unsympathetic. She has never agreed that raising girls in ignorance was doing them any favours; she disapproves of Dolly's parents and their deep and thorough liking for the euphemistic side of life.

"Goodness, child — what did you expect? You went alone with a man to a hotel room! Did you think he'd offer you a cup of tea and send you on your way?"

Dolly listens to the speech that follows, as Auntie Dee pours out her venom against men, and Dolly understands why Auntie Dee has never married, has never had a beau. "They're all *bastards*," she pants, circling Dolly, like an angry vulture, "and they never live up to their obligations! Look at your poor mother! Slaving for him like an Irish washerwoman!"

Dolly has never seen her mother slave and doubts if her mother would even know how; their meals are prepared by a black cook whom Dolly sees infrequently but who sings Jamaican songs lustily behind the kitchen door. The laundry gets sent out to Bergmann's every Monday and Friday, and Shipley's sends a skinny boy to bring the groceries round. Dolly isn't sure how anyone could slave under such circumstances, but Auntie Dee is determined. With a final flourish, she tears the cover off her latest work: a naked man, crucified upon a woman, hanging upside down like some grotesque illustration from the *Kama Sutra*.

Dolly thinks she can see Roy Farber in his pinched, wan features, the way his baggy underpants cleave to his bony hips. She thinks about Roy Farber and his suitcase full of Bibles, and the bellhop at the hotel, and Roy's lurid stories of the great metropolis. She thinks she doesn't want to be like Auntie Dee, but neither does she want to be like her mother, forced to pick at chicken torsos in the holy presence of the Reverend Friday. Dolly thinks she might find herself another man one of these days, with a suitcase full of Bibles and the inclination to show Roy Farber just a little thing or two.

Martha and Johnnie

Here are Martha and Johnnie in a snapshot taken by a friend at the Episcopal Garden Party many years ago — in that era that we suppose was more wholesome and more simple, that led our grandmothers and great-grandmothers to give themselves in marriage to men they hardly knew and didn't love. We don't do that anymore — we don't throw ourselves away — but how to explain the classmate who, pregnant with twins at seventeen, marries the man with nothing to his credit but several pairs of shoes and a room in his mother's house? We already know the outcome: he will come scratching and blinking out of a shadowy back bedroom each morning, shirtless and in underpants, his breath smelling sour, like old milk, the hair under his arms standing out in aggrieved tufts. His mother will make him breakfast, as his new wife stumbles to the bathroom and vomits noisily into the toilet. She will never be smart enough, clean enough or subservient enough for her mother-in-law, and when the children are born, they will be at once appropriated by his mother, and cooed and fussed over as though he had produced them himself. His teenage wife will become merely part of the background, an afterthought, unable to broach the paired divinity of mother and son.

But all that is in the future, and anyway, this is not what happened to Martha and Johnnie, for theirs is a love story from the very beginning and has remained so — at least that's how I see it. Martha lived in a very fine white house with her grandmother — a house with a sun porch where she might go on fine days to read a book. The windows were crowned with delicate lace curtains, and the garden at the back was laid with carefully articulated beds of flowers. Martha's grandmother had been married to a former telegraph boy, a late bloomer who went on to make his fortune in the silver mines of Nevada. He'd come back East, to Baltimore, and built or bought this fine house on a quiet street in a quality neighbourhood.

Martha's parents died young, of polio caught while swimming, and Martha's grandmother has raised her to believe in their memories as articles of faith. Martha's grandmother believes in marrying for love, insofar as social customs allow, and indeed, she herself married her telegraph boy for love. Martha has no intention of falling in love, but if she did, it would not be with the telegraph boy. Martha is happy at home with Grandma, reading books and dreaming out the window as she watches the snow fall. Every other morning at precisely nine-thirty, the young man who brings the coal (for Grandma, mindful of waste, only ever buys coal in pre-selected and carefully measured amounts) appears at the back door and rings the bell that is installed there for just that purpose. Johnnie Bates wouldn't dream of going to the front door, having the niceties of decorum hammered into him by his father whose name was not always Bates, but Brodski, but that was many years ago. Johnnie Bates is about Martha's height, with brown eyes and rosy cheeks, and if you look closely at the photograph, you will see that there is something keen and self-determined in his eyes. He will not be dismissed, and even though he knows his station and is mindful of his place, he is determined to rise above it. Perhaps he will learn the coal business well and become a rich entrepreneur. He is twenty years old now, and Martha is seventeen, and anything is possible, anything at all, especially since it's Martha who answers the bell, who directs him as to the proper placement of the coal — Martha who watches the play of his strong muscles underneath a cotton shirt, black with coal dust. It's Martha who sees that, although his hands are roughened from hard labour, they are fine and well-groomed, the nails kept short and neat. Martha studies him, the strong bow of his back, the muscles of his thighs, as he pours the coal out of its sack, and she wonders what it would feel like to be touched by those hands, and she knows enough of worldly things to realize that this isn't love, or anything like it.

"You're all set, now then." Johnnie Bates says this every other day as he brings the coal and tips his cap to Martha and to her grandmother, who is watching carefully from the kitchen door. The old lady only seems benign and comforting; if Johnnie Bates made one unsanctioned move towards her granddaughter, the old woman would thrash him. Johnnie knows this, and it is why he confines himself to looking, to smiling and tipping his hat, to pretending a lower-class humility that does not exist in him. He knows, because his father has told him, that such behaviour is expected, but if he watches and listens carefully, and waits his turn, he may reap anything he wants. So Johnnie is content to gaze at the lovely turn of Martha's ankles, the coral ring upon her hand, the swell of her breasts. He is content to bide his time.

Johnnie and his father live alone in a red brick house by the rail yard. It isn't so bad, except when the trains come through, and all the dishes in the cupboards rattle. Once a blue and white vase belonging to Johnnie's mother fell off the sideboard and broke. "She brought this all the way from Warsaw," his father said, trying unsuccessfully to paste it together, later that night. "It was my first gift to her when we were courting, and now look at it — smashed." His father was very distraught. "The one thing she brought from Warsaw." Johnnie tried to comfort his father, leading him over to the table for some tea, clearing away the bits of broken pottery.

Johnnie's father is big-boned, big-bodied and slow moving, like a bull. His shoulders are permanently stooped, the result of years of carrying heavy bags of coal. Johnnie tries to imagine his father next to Martha — his big, gruff, kindly father next to Martha — but it is an incongruous picture. He loves his father dearly, fiercely, with the kind of savage and protective love that boys normally direct toward their mothers. He thinks he would kill to protect the old man, to keep him from harm. He cannot bear to think of anyone making fun of his father, of his thick accent, or the way he walks with his shoulders stooped, his trousers bagged at the knees and backside. When they go to the open-air market on Friday afternoons, Johnnie shepherds his father along, his hand hovering protectively near his elbow. He sees the grey in the older man's hair, the liver spots on the backs of his hands, and feels as though his heart were being strangled in a vise. "You always have to check the fish," his father is in the habit of saying, "Get your nose down there real close. It might *look* okay, but looking don't mean *bupkes.*"

His father glories in the sights and sounds of the market, the fruit stalls and fishmongers, the fresh vegetables. There is a particular stall with three Amish men, and he always stops to talk to them — Johnnie muses that Pa might find something vaguely rabbinical in their dark hats and long beards, something that comforts him. Johnnie joins in the prayers at Temple for his father's sake, not because he is religious. The old man clings to their Jewishness, but Johnnie has discarded it as something belonging to the old country, something out of place in Baltimore.

And what of Martha, what is she thinking all this time that Johnnie comes to carry the coal? Martha has been reading pulp novels and serial romances in the ladies' magazines and wondering about the man she will marry. She still answers the ring when Johnnie comes by in the mornings, and she still watches carefully as he unloads the coal. "You sure are pretty," Johnnie says to her one morning. Martha is shocked and a little angry that someone like him should presume to speak to her (already, at this early stage of life, she is giving herself airs), but when she complains to her grandmother, the old woman laughs at her. Airs and graces are all very well and good, she tells Martha, but a husband is a husband.

Johnnie tells his father about Martha as they eat supper together at night. He tells his father that he is going to marry Martha, and the old man nods solemnly. "Of course you will," his father says, "but are you going to bring her here, to this house, this place? Is this any way to treat your bride?" Johnnie thinks that perhaps he will get a railway job, but even as he says this, he knows he cannot leave his father to run their coal business alone. He looks at his father's gnarled fingers, the shoulders that are stooped from the burdens of a lifetime, and he knows he cannot abandon his father. Nothing is ever said, but both father and son recognize that the idea is dead. Later, Johnnie's father is sitting on the back porch, watching the trains roll into the railway yard, and Johnnie comes out to join him.

They watch the trains for a moment in silence, and then his father says, "That's what you gotta do — build yourself up in business, make some money for that girl of yours." Johnnie isn't sure what his father is saying and doesn't want to ask. He sits beside him for a long time, listening to the clash and clank of trains being run into the yard. He watches as darkness falls and the first fireflies come out. He thinks about Martha with mingled happiness and dread.

The seasons wear away, and for a while neither Martha nor her grandmother buy coal. When autumn comes, Johnnie goes again to the white house, rings at the back door. He waits a long time before a blond man in an ill-fitting suit opens the door. He stares at Johnnie with his bucket of coal, his mouth opening and closing on nothing. "Delivery," Johnnie says stupidly, peering past the blond man, staring at the mass of people milling about inside the house, staring at the floral wreaths and the candles. He realizes that he has stumbled in on a funeral. It occurs to him that Martha must have died — all these long months that he has not seen her, she has contracted some illness and died.

"Are you all right?" The blond man takes Johnnie by the arm, sits him in a chair and fetches a glass of water.

"What did she die of?" It's imperative that he know.

"Tuberculosis," the blond man says. "Everything considered, she went very quick — which is a good thing, at her age."

"At her *age?*" Johnnie is incredulous. "She was no more than seventeen!"

The blond man stares at him. "*Seventeen?* She was eighty if she was a day!" It strikes him that Johnnie has made a false assumption. "Old Aggie was eighty — you didn't think —"

Martha appears in the doorway, beautiful in simple mourning black. The blond man is talking, but Johnnie hears nothing, sees nothing except Martha. When his hands close over hers, everything else is blotted out, the whole world and everything in it entirely captured in his Martha's sweet taken breath.

I love you, he thinks. *I love you more than anything.*

The Opium Lady

Here is Jesse, an actress in vaudeville — exquisitely pretty and poised, and looking very like a confection with her real silk parasol and her orchid corsage. She is having her picture taken, to be made into calling cards that she can hand out to gentlemen of her choice. Every night, after her performance, there are dozens of roses waiting in her dressing room backstage. She knows some of the names on the cards, but others are strangers, and she wonders what they must be like, judging by their names. Jesse knows that these men send her flowers because, watching her from the other side of the footlights, in the dancehall crowded with the faintly-sweaty scent of other bodies, they each believe they can possess her — for an evening, perhaps a weekend, or longer. Each man in the audience thinks that she is his alone, believes that her glance lights on him because he finds him somehow desirable. They have all formed their own opinions as to what she's really like, and these speculations range from the puerile to the depraved. Always there is an element of sex, and this is not entirely unfounded, for, at the very end of her act, Jesse performs a fan dance, somewhat in the style of Josephine Baker, minus the bananas. Always the giant feather fans dip and whirl, flashing the tantalizing intimation of flesh, the curve of a breast or buttock, but never revealing anything of substance. Such a display drives men mad with desire, and Jesse knows this, revels in it. She needs to have them eating out of the palm of her hand — she needs to draw them to her on their knees as they mop their sweaty foreheads, eager — *panting* — for the proverbial glimpse of stocking, a waft of what lies underneath her dress. Jesse enjoys this attention, and will sometimes have dinner with any of these men, or allow them to escort her dancing, but she never allows a man to touch her beyond taking her arm. Once, a man she was with, an undergraduate, touched her lightly between the shoulder blades as they were exiting a taxi — Jesse turned on him, furious and spitting, her green eyes flashing like an angry cat. He had only touched her for the merest part of a second, just above the luxurious sweep of her fur stole — no more than a moment's touch, a moment's chance. It was as if his fingertips had *branded* her somehow, and Jesse cannot bear that. To be branded is to be owned, and she will not be owned by any man. This is the key to her survival: being able to order her life any way she wants it, without fear of censure, with the paternalistic concern that most men would exhibit, given half a chance.

Jesse is starring in a rather grotesque vaudeville production called *The Opium Lady* — about a spinster who attracts many beaus and then kills them all with opium. This, with great hi-jinks and resultant hilarity. Jesse plays it very comedic, all kiss curls and big Betty Boop eyes. Underneath the facade of the ingenue, however, is a slow-growing identification: every night that Jesse goes onstage, she feels as if she is becoming Lillian, her character in the show — every night, she sees the lurid, panting faces of the men in the audience, their expressions of open-mouthed lust during her finale: the lascivious shoulder-shaking, bosom-jiggling dance. She feels that she is *becoming* Lillian: the climactic scene where she administers the overdose to her last and latest beau provokes a keen thrill. She lives for the moment when Lillian passes out the poisoned wine, when they all drink, when they all die. Jesse finds herself watching the actors' faces eagerly, as though a glance from her could truly make it poisoned wine, could effect that metamorphosis. She stands with fists clenched, sweat running down her arms, hoping — but of course it's only a play, and anyway, she has no opium to hand. She performs her dance in a kind of nervous frenzy, moving wildly, allowing the audience to see more than she ever has before. She returns to her dressing room, sweaty and exhausted, finds a line of men waiting in the hallway — men of all shapes and sizes, men of all persuasions, all walks of life. For a perfunctory fee, they can have her every night — have her in their minds, in every way they can imagine. There are flowers, of course, from men she knows and those she doesn't. There are always flowers, every night.

She is looking at herself in the mirror as she takes her makeup off, listening to the rumble of the men outside her door. Her fists are clenching and unclenching and, on impulse, she rips open the door and selects a man at random: Peter Biedermeyer, a florist with sweaty palms and thick spectacles, the archetypal fall guy. She grabs him and kisses him in front of the rest, who whistle and exclaim. "Go on home!" she tells them, "I've got the one I want!" She herds Biedermeyer into her dressing room, pours herself a Scotch, and lights a thick cigar, ignoring Biedermeyer, who is entranced by the sway of her unbound breasts beneath her silk kimono. She eats, drinks, smokes, talks on the telephone, examines her legs for bruises, and picks her teeth — all while Biedermeyer watches. Finally, she asks him how much money he's got, because she wants to get a bite to eat, "Somewhere nice," she tells him, "not one of these hash joints."

Biedermeyer is not what he seems — nobody is. He isn't stupid, or at least, not as stupid as Jesse thinks he is, and her body, her beauty, doesn't dazzle him. He watches her critically, noting her extreme self-absorption. He's met other women like her — in fact, he makes it his business to meet women like Jesse. He's been waiting a long time, and he has sent dozens of gifts, expensive Godiva chocolates, flowers, and jewellery — all in an attempt to get Jesse's attention. Jesse may think that she selected him randomly, but this isn't so, for Biedermeyer fancies himself something of a Don Juan and believes that the exertion of his charms is the thing that made her choose him. The commonality between them is, of course, cherished delusion.

Biedermeyer calls for a taxi at the curb, while Jesse waits, wrapped in fur and gorgeously aloof. She sneers when Biedermeyer hails the cab: "Ain't you got a car of your own, sport?" But she gets into the cab with him, sits silently smoking and gazing out the window. Biedermeyer takes advantage of the darkness to gaze at her, watching the play of passing street lights against the line of her jaw — he notices that her face is getting a little slack underneath the chin, and he wonders how old she is. He knows nothing about her, beyond the facts printed on her press sheet, and this tells him nothing at all. He wants to see life from behind her eyes, but he already knows that Jesse lives in monochrome. The joy has gone out of life for her.

Jesse originally comes from Hagersfield, the only child of a white woman and a migrant worker. She has never known her father, as he stayed just long enough to get Jesse's mother pregnant before moving on. Jesse's mother has often told her stories about him, how he loved to play the guitar, and how he was very musical. Jesse's mother always thought this was a great thing, and pushed her daughter to take roles in the Sunday school pageant and the Passion play at Easter. She was convinced that Jesse could be like her father, more than her father, and more than her mother, too. In her mind, this half-forgotten Mexican is a great entertainer, a Sammy Davis Junior or an Al Jolson, and she wants Jesse to be like him. Jesse, on the other hand, is a mediocre actress who can't sing, who can barely dance, who has no real talent. She met a travelling vaudeville barker at Hagersfield's one and only tavern, the Town Pump, when she was sixteen, and ran away with him. He took her virginity in a motel room just off Route 1, and when she woke up he was gone. He left a twenty-dollar bill on her naked back.

But Jesse was undaunted and bummed a ride to Baltimore, moved in with Jacky Bustamente, a theatre and girlie-bar owner, and probably a pimp. She pestered him for singing lessons, dancing lessons, voice and elocution. She cut her long hair off, and wears it bobbed now, with a saucy kiss-curl, like Theda Bara. It was Bustamente who first put her on the stage, but Jesse was not an immediate hit. Even now, she frequently forgets the words of the song she's supposed to be singing, and the audience will boo and hiss, laughing at her. When this happens, she feels as if she's choking, as if she's smothering, and the audience recedes through the layers of noise and smoke, until she's all alone.

"What did you do after Bustamente?" Biedermeyer's voice breaks in upon her thoughts, and Jesse realizes that she has been reminiscing aloud. She is still in a taxi with Biedermeyer, and they are far out in the country, the lights of Baltimore disappearing in the rear-view mirror.

"Hey! This ain't no eatin' place! I thought I told you —"

"We'll be there soon," he says, and reaches across to pat her hand. It's a measure of her emotional distraction that she lets him.

Jesse watches out the window as the forest grows up around them, and she begins to feel afraid. Where is Biedermeyer taking her, and why? Perhaps a little, out-of-the-way crab shack, she reasons. She pulls a flask out of her purse and takes a long pull, wondering if Biedermeyer will expect her to stay the night, wondering where she can get more gin. She expects that Biedermeyer will expect the same sorts of things that her other suitors have expected. She drifts away, into an uneasy sleep, lulled by the sound of the tires on the roadway. She dreams that she is onstage at Carnegie Hall, but the audience is full of women, all the women she has ever known, multiplied many times over, all staring at her with something like awe, all clapping and cheering wildly, throwing bouquets of roses that rain down on the stage.

She awakens with a jolt as the taxi pulls to a halt in front of a small shack, lit from within. The shack is by itself in a grove of pines, as though it had sprung out of the ground, unaided. But there are various cars and trucks parked about the perimeter, and a mule is tethered to a hitching post just beside the door. It must be some sort of eating place.

Biedermeyer takes her inside, and Jesse realizes with horror that it's some sort of church. The parishioners are of the inevitable variety of poor whites — people from the tiny towns all along this desolate stretch of road, all the way down to where the Patuxent River meets the Chesapeake. They nod politely to her as Biedermeyer manoeuvres her into a chair.

No one seems to recognize her. No one knows who she is. Jesse remembers being at this kind of service in her childhood, and she is able to sing most of the hymns from memory. Now she is in her element: now she can settle comfortably into her *métier*. She turns to flash a smile at Biedermeyer.

And then they bring the boxes out — wooden boxes, rough-hewn with several small holes drilled into them. When Biedermeyer opens the lid and hands her the snake, Jesse finally and unequivocally screams. She turns to flee, but Biedermeyer holds her arm, will not let her go. She can see the snake's tiny glistening eyes, its wicked forked tongue, the visage of the Devil. Her insides are a quaking cavity of fear, her armpits running with a copious sweat. She wrenches away from Biedermeyer and flees into the darkness, running down the narrow dirt road, running back to Baltimore and the endless line of men outside her door.

The Goose Girls

The Hayter sisters live on a dirt farm in Southern Maryland; they were raised by their daddy, after their momma left, and they have always been called 'The Goose Girls' because of the various cackling noises they make when they are together. This picture was taken late in summer, with Irene, the eldest, all got up in slacks. Their father had borrowed some money from the Hedges, and he took the girls for a weekend trip down to the Outer Banks. They were fascinated by the coastline and the lighthouse; Helen said she would marry a lighthouse keeper when she grew up, and she would climb the stairs into the wooden tower to see the light go around. Nobody back in Hagersfield would believe it this if they saw it: the Goose Girls on a holiday somewhere besides down the road. Nobody would say anything out loud, but you know they're thinking it. You know they're thinking nasty things and saying them, inside the privacy of their own heads.

They love the summertime, these Goose Girls, and look forward to getting out of school so they can be free: away from the sterile confines of the schoolroom and Miss Lamar the teacher with her chalky-dry fingers, poking accusations at their narrow ribs. *You ain't nothin' but trash, girl.* Everybody knows about them, here in Hagersfield, and everybody knows why their momma left their daddy, why she up and ran away and left him all alone. Zeb Hayter never did have the sense God gave him, and Lord knows how he manages with those three girls. The town itself is poor, even as the rest of the country seems to prosper; Time and all the flashy greatness of past economic boom has left Hagersfield behind. And Daddy is a dirt farmer, through no fault of his own, but this is Hayter land, and damned if he won't find some way to make something of it. He's been trying thirty years.

Daddy is a kind man, not very bright, who knuckled under the perishing admonitions of Miss Lamar the schoolteacher, and managed to get Grade Six. He can barely do his sums, owing to his bad eyesight, and he cuts wood in the hillsides up near Butlerville, drags it on his back for miles and sells it in the town, going door to door, and ever so polite. *Firewood, ma'am? Got me a nice dry bit of timber here.* If he's defeated by his life, it's his own fault, but such a pity and a shame Miz Sally Hayter up and left him. When he tucks the children in at night he makes them say their prayers, and tells them, "Pray for Momma's soul up there in Heaven, up there with Jesus." Irene is the oldest, a tomboy who likes wearing slacks instead of dresses, but growing up real nice, considering. Irene remembers Momma, and after all the lights are out and Daddy's sitting on the porch alone, she tells the other sisters stories. "Listen here," Irene says, shifting in the bed so she's lying on her elbow, "I remember Momma when y'all don't, and I remember the time she dove into Jacob's Creek and sove old Mister Bayles from drowning. She drug him round the neck and hauled him up on land, and he was spewing water from his nose, his eyes and his mouth. Momma got a medal from the President." Momma becomes gigantic and heroic, looming through the cold half-light on legs as large as stanchions. Another time, Irene tells them how Momma drove an ambulance in France during the War, and saved untold hundreds of soldiers from a plague of fiery lightning, driving up into the hills until the danger had passed. The girls can't get enough of it and beg Irene to tell them more, and afterwards Irene will lie awake listening to the gentle breathing of her sisters and imagine furious adventures that cannot possibly stand up in the light of day. Daddy met Momma on the bridge in San Francisco, and Momma was lovely in the sunshine and the wind, standing atop steel girders with the sea breeze rippling through her long dark hair, a silk scarf around her throat, her arms outstretched like some fantastic bird. Perhaps Momma could fly, and that's what she was doing up there on the bridge, trying to fly, and Daddy came and took her down to earth, and Momma never flew again. This is how they met, in the midst of Momma's short, arrested flight.

This is how the Goose Girls grow, lying in the dark and listening to fantastic stories while Daddy sits out on the porch, smoking in the cricket song and breathing out the stars. By the time Irene is twenty, Daddy has died (a heart attack up on Prosser's Mountain, chopping wood to sell or burn), and Helen is the one who reminisces about their mother's death. Helen remembers it always in the context of their father's, as though the two were bound absolutes, crushed together in some obscure dance and weighted there by gravity. "Momma just went away one night," Helen tells them. "There was no fighting, no shouting. She just up and went." There is something savage in this, and indeed, Helen says these things as she is sitting in the semi-dark of Wayley's Funeral Home, sitting in the direct stream of the corpse's chilly breath. A clutch of people wander by the opened door, and Helen starts up out of her chair, catching the tail-end of a phrase, *old whore*, and goes instead to gaze down at her father in his coffin.

His hair is black as night, unsilvered by the passage of time, and though his hands are gnarled with a lifetime's worth of work, his face is strangely passive, entirely in repose, as though the silenced brain within were meditating on some great existential question. He told them all a story once, a fairy tale, "The Goose Girl," about a child who lived in a hut in the forest with a woodsman who loved her. And then a handsome prince came and drew the goose girl up onto his horse, and they were never seen again. Helen now wonders where they went, but when she goes to ask Irene, she cannot find either of her sisters, and she is left alone there: alone in that small room, alone in Wayley's Funeral Home . . . alone with her father's mortal shell.

She thinks about Momma, striding through the forest on legs as strong and firm as stanchions. She thinks about Momma, on the bridge in San Francisco, trying not to fly. She sees a picture of them, standing stiff and rigid in the wedding clothes, their faces paused in expressions of delight, curiously still. She sees herself and Pearl and Irene, standing in the summer grass in front of some old lighthouse. In these memories, everything is just the same as always, Momma is still gone, and Irene tells them fantastic stories in the night. But no one saw Momma die, and no one knows if she only went away or was spirited to some obscure region on the back of a princely stallion. Helen wants to ask them, but no one can tell her. No one wants to open those old wounds again.

She finds Irene and Pearl, trails them to their hiding place by virtue of the hanging cloud of smoke. They are sharing a cigarette in the cloying heat, crouched behind the funeral home, their faces carefully averted. They have nothing now to say to each other. Irene has found a job in New York City, making paper hats in a great factory along the Hudson, and Pearl is married to a drunken Pennsylvania Dutchman. They both pretend happiness. Helen stayed in Hagersfield, and looks after the aged Miss Lamar, her chalky fingers now contracted back into her palms like ancient talons. Even Daddy drifted by them, somehow, in the intervening years, and on the day he died Helen was down in Miss Lamar's basement, cleaning up some pickle jars, listening to the angry sound of Miss Lamar's cane as it poked into the floor. It was a hot day, some said over a hundred, and Daddy up on Prosser's Mountain all alone, heaving his axe into the cowering trees, shedding sweat around him then like raindrops. Helen can't imagine that he understood; probably he thought it was his stomach, or he'd strained a muscle in his back, heaving his axe around up there. Irene was in New York City, making paper hats and Christmas crackers, those little paper tubes with jewellery inside, bits of things and trinkets, noisemakers and shiny cardboard horns for New Year's Eve. Pearl was tending house for her husband Johnny, dithering her way from room to room, commenting to herself and him about the state of things, tripping over empty bottles. Daddy was away, was far away, and even Helen hardly gave a thought to him. Joe Bob Mac came and told her, *Miz Hayter your daddy's dead*, and she'd dropped a jar of pickle juice and felt the chilly prickle of splashed vinegar seeping through her stockings. Joe Bob was too tall to fit down Miz Lamar's dark basement, and so he crouched upon the wooden stairs and called it down to her, *Miz Hayter your daddy's dead*. It was as if everything stopped just for a moment, as though the planet paused its turning through the stars and things and people lost their hold and floated just above the surface of the earth. And then a noisy cough from Miss Lamar, and Joe Bob lifting up his cap to her as his long back disappeared into uncertain daylight.

"Nobody ever told us the truth," Helen watches Pearl and Irene smoking, notices the furtive expressions on their faces, as though they'd been caught in a lie, accused of some unwieldy deed. "About Momma or Daddy."

"Don't bring that up." It is Irene who speaks, crushing out the dying cigarette beneath her heel, blinking at Helen like some strange species of bird. "What's past is past." She glances at Pearl, making sure. Helen feels that she is withering beneath their gaze.

"All those stories —"

"They were nothing but stories, Helen. Just lies and nonsense. Stuff to keep the ghosts away — don't you know anything?" Irene's upper lip is curled, a curiously canine gesture, and her thin hands are crushing her handbag. She doesn't want to talk about this; she only came here out of respect for Daddy. She wants him put into the ground so she can get on with things, get back on the bus, head back to the city. She doesn't want to linger here, amidst the stench of magnolia and pine, the air clotted and sticky with old words. This isn't her life anymore.

"I only wanted to know about Momma. About Daddy." Helen is seven years old again, asking them for something, caught between them, lingering in hope. "I wanted to know where Momma went, how come she left Daddy. I'm not digging — honest, I'm not."

"What's past is past," Irene says with finality. Gathering her handbag and the sagging ankles of her stockings, she pushes past them, head and shoulders down, disappears into the front door of the funeral home, goes to wait attendance on her father's corpse. Pearl follows, trailing in her wake like bubbles from a passing ship, vanishing with Irene into silence. Helen is left alone.

She leans against the painted clapboard of Wayley's Funeral Home and tries to summon up some tears for Daddy, but her eyes are dry. She thinks about the wild stories Irene used to tell, those majestic tales of Momma, and it occurs to her that she cannot mourn her parents because she never knew them. Daddy is the beloved woodsman, she and her sisters the Goose Girls, but Momma is the unknown knight-at-arms, striding through the clinging thicket of the forest, whacking out the obstacles with the bright sword of her legend. If no one knows what truly became of her, then perhaps she is still living, somewhere.

Somewhere inside the clapboard walls, the funeral begins.

The Butcher Boys

Here is a picture of Roy and Donald, standing side-by-side in their uniforms, all tricked out to go and fight the Germans or the Japanese. It must be summertime, because the trees are very much in leaf, and Roy and Donald have their sleeves rolled up. Also, they are squinting into the camera and therefore into the sun, which they would not do if it were cloudy. But I think it must be the end of summer, rather than a month like June, because the quality of light is hazy and doesn't have the sharp brightness of the high point of the year. I think there might be a field behind them, somewhere in the distance, just beyond the wall. There might be a meadow there, a place to sit and rest, a picnic spot.

Donald is the taller of the two, and his arm — the one showing in the photograph — is bent behind his body in such a way that it looks like just the stump of an arm — as though it had been amputated as the result of some accident. This is not a recent mishap, for the stump (if it is a stump and not merely a hidden arm) is cleanly healed.

But there's a curious sort of gloss over them both, as if they had been removed from some other, easygoing sort of place and dropped down upon this lawn in Hagersfield, completely unexpected. The inscription on the back of the photograph says "high school boy friends — 1940," but this is not to suggest that Roy and Donald ever enjoyed anything except a friendly wrestling match once in a while, and certainly, times were simpler then. This is not what concerns me, not at all: rather, the date, that earnest "1940" which signals the threshold of America's first cautious foray into World War Two. Indeed, there is a very slight smudge of darkness between the two of them, occupying the space a third body might have claimed. This is where Terry might have been, except he's dead — just as Roy and Donald will be, once the European war gets its teeth into them.

Roy and Donald have a secret pact, however, despite their sunny, boyish natures, and it is this: they have sworn deeds of great heroics to each other, and often, after a Coke and fries, they regale themselves with tales of derring-do, of glorious defiance in the face of war. Roy and Donald cannot see the shadowy thing that occupies the space beside Donald's elbow. They see all of it as a great exercise in heroism; they cannot possibly understand that both of them will see action in the Pacific, be torpedoed and sunk, and both will drown — ignominiously, as other men in other wars have drowned.

At the very edge of the field behind them, (this field that must be there, I know it) there is a small tarpaper shack. You can't see the shack in the photo, but believe me it exists, and Roy and Donald have been there many times together. The shack is built next to an old tobacco barn, and houses Old Sukey who isn't really all that old, and whose name isn't really Sukey, but this is what she has been named, and somehow it sticks to her like dirt or moisture.

When Roy and Donald were born, Old Sukey was there, tending to their mothers in the old way, seeing that the clothes were loosened, that no cats were present, and that all the doors and windows in the house were open. It made no nevermind that nobody ever invited Sukey — if there was an impending birth, death or calving, then Sukey came, because she knew about it, because the spirits told her. No one was really sure where Old Sukey had come from, although some said she'd been a *voudoun* priestess down in Haiti, or a witch woman on the bayou in Louisiana. Mr. Hedge, who owns the store in town, says that he'd known Old Sukey's grandmother, and she was from Jamaica, and that was how Sukey knew the magic. The curious thing is that Sukey — despite what you might think — is white. Neither Roy nor Donald in their cleverness can explain this. Also, Sukey has long red hair and brown eyes, and does not sound remotely like a person from Jamaica. But there can be no other explanation for the dubious magic that Old Sukey knows, and Roy and Donald pretend to themselves (and to anyone who will listen) that it doesn't matter. Roy and Donald go to visit Sukey when the moon is waning, because this is when Sukey will be putting up great batches of the flaming firewater that she makes, this backwoods *aqua vitae*. In exchange for their respectful attention to her stories, Roy and Donald can expect a shot glass full of Sukey's potent home-brew — and a look into their futures. Sukey does this by staring at the white spots on their fingernails until Roy and Donald are quaking with fright, certain that Sukey sees either a violent death, or worse — a life of ease and cowardice. They sit in silence while she reads their fingernails, heads reeling and breath sour with the stench of Sukey's home brew. They go back to her time and time again, hoping that she will reveal some glorious destiny, but she never does. "Commonplace," she always mutters, tossing their hands back into their laps. "G'wan, git out my house!" They scurry away obediently, not daring to speak of their fear. They know that if they can endure the mystery of Sukey Sykes, they can outlive the war.

But they aren't really afraid of Sukey — not Old Sukey, who attended both their mothers in childbed. And anyway, Old Sukey can't tell them anything that they don't already know — and if she's such a good fortune teller, how come she isn't rich and famous? How come she lives in that old tarpaper shack, and sits with women who are having babies, and how come Sukey never says anything about the war?

Here is a picture of Roy and Donald, squinting into the late-summer sun. Donald's arm looks like it might be amputated below the elbow, but everybody here in Hagersfield knows that when his body washed ashore near Guam, he was as whole and as complete as on the day he was born.

Neither Do They Spin

Mrs. Mellicant lives in Baltimore, a widow and the aunt of the Goose Girls, the Hayter sisters of Hagersfield. Mrs. Mellicant grew up in Hagersfield, but left when she got married — moved on, really, from that lonesome backwater, on to better things. Mr. Mellicant came down Hagersfield way on a trip through southern Maryland, and before you knew it, there he was on Hattie Bayles's doorstep, with his hat in his hand, asking if please ma'am might Patience come out walking with him. He was twenty-five in those days, lean and spare as a fiddle bow, with enough hair oil that you'd think he was some kind of Arab. His nose was long and thin, and he always seemed to be asking you a question, even when he wasn't saying anything at all, given how his eyebrows rose up into his hairline. He had long, thin hands, too, like that piano player Hattie knew up in Richmond, that Yankee with the red hair. But he kept himself very clean and his fingernails were short, and he didn't have a moustache — that was most important. Hattie Bayles didn't hold with men having hair on their faces, thinking that it made them seem too much like monkeys. Old

Jeb Bayles, now, he had no beard or moustache, but when he washed himself underneath the backyard pump in the afternoons, the hair on his back made a kind of sweater for him. Hattie never said nothing about men having hair on their bodies, only that it was the way God made 'em.

Patience Bayles was a tiny little bit of a thing in those days: petite and slender, with a waist a man could wrap his hands around and have his fingers meet behind. She wore a size three shoe, but for all her diminutive size, she clattered imperiously about the house on little dolly feet, forever screeching and clacking like a backed-up sink. She wouldn't let Mr. Mellicant so much as kiss her hand, and even after they were married for awhile, she called him Mr. Mellicant in public and in private, not thinking it fitting that a lady should address a gentleman by his Christian name. Mrs. Mellicant believed in dignity and composure, as dictated by the scions of her society, the Junior League, the First Families of Virginia. Her mother's antecedents had come over many, many years before with Baltimore, crossing the treacherous Atlantic on the *Ark* and the *Dove*. When they first set foot upon the hallowed ground of North America, some went to Virginia and some stayed in Maryland, and the two sides have hated each other ever since. Hattie thought it was a shame that you had to be unkind to kin, but facts were facts, and didn't Lester Bayles swindle Grandma out of her life's savings? Still and all, the Bayles's were of ancient stock, first settlers in a new and hostile land, and Hattie was determined that no one should forget it. A suitable interval must pass before Patience can allow young Mr. Mellicant and his ubiquitous hair oil into their front parlour, and indeed, it was a suitable interval: Mr. Mellicant made seven more trips to Hagersfield before Hattie Bayles would let him past the screen porch, and only then if he removed his hat. Young Mr. Mellicant was a romantic at heart, that's what Miz Bayles told the neighbours and the ladies at the church. He was forever bringing flowers, fancy boxes of candy done up in paper hearts, and once, some kind of sparkling apple cider that fizzed and popped like cola. He said he'd got it up Philadelphia way, when he was passing through there on his travels, for Mr. Mellicant was an accountant of some note, and frequently did the books for several import-ant businesses all along the eastern seaboard. It was this that finally tipped Hattie Bayles in his favour: the fact that he had a useful calling and didn't set himself to decorate the front porch of his momma's house, like so many of the young 'uns did nowadays. He had a purpose, was eminently useful insofar as his business was conducted in the province of men behind closed doors and in dusty offices in the city. Miz Bayles didn't hold with gentlemen airing their professions in the presence of ladies; it wasn't fitting. Only with great difficulty did she consent to Patience's taking Mr. Mellicant's hand, his hair oil and his name, and with due ceremony they were wed — a springtime wedding, in the little church that had stood on land sacred to the Bayleses for more than three hundred years. Once this had been accomplished, Hattie considered that her duty to her daughter had been done, and she turned her back on Patience Mellicant and her husband. It was only fitting, after all: no *proper* mother would condescend to involve herself in her married daughter's life, and Patience had her own row to hoe, now that the deed was done. She could not know that Edwin Mellicant was essentially a dry and desiccated man once the business of courting was done, one whose fundamental human emotions were much sapped by the passage of the years.

Mrs. Mellicant isn't unhappy, quite the opposite, for she has entrenched herself firmly in her own life. She is very active in the Presbyterian Church (even though Mellicant, when she married him, was Catholic) and has an extensive circle of very dear friends. Once a week, she gets together with them, and they knit for the church: socks, mittens and great, loose-limbed scarves whose stitches barely hang together. These garments are collected by some nameless, formless woman in a grey dress, and brought about the poorer neighbourhoods of Baltimore, to be given to the "coloured people." Mrs. Mellicant has never actually *met* any of the "coloured people" but she is certain, in the most secret regions of her soul, that they are most eminently needful of her charity, and this knowledge lends a certain backwashed piety to her knitting, and speeds her fingers through the endless hours of tea and idle chatter. She is proud of being able to "do her duty to society" but neverthe-less dislikes the idea of the coloureds wearing what she makes. If she imagines that her midnight-blue mittens might one day grace the grasping paws of some darky or his wife or the end-less monkey children that lie scattered all around their hovel, she shudders, hardly daring to lift another stitch. She tells Eliza Swift one day, "They're not like us, you know," and of course Eliza agrees with her, for what else could she do? Here is the dividing line: the line of demarcation between Mrs. Mellicant and Eliza Swift and the lesser races, the dark tide that forever laps its hungry lips against the shoreline of humanity. "Give them an inch and they'll take a yard," Eliza Swift agrees, pouring tea into china cups so delicate that you can see the daylight through the patterns of their damask roses.

Mrs. Mellicant has no clear ideas about bigotry and wouldn't know enough to call it by its proper name. Her prejudice is of the most benign sort, utterly unaware of itself, and softened somewhat by her innate benevolence, which spreads outwards from itself, seeking others. Here is her photograph, and there she stands, stalwart and ready for anything, her hands decorously in her pockets, her feet struggling with the sand below. She belongs to a different age, a time when "po' white trash," those people living in places as obscure and deadly as Mudlick Holler, could count themselves above the coloureds. This isn't something that her consciousness needs ponder, it's just the way things are, and Mrs. Mellicant would never think to question it. But she has seen the rise of the coloureds right here in Baltimore, whereas when she was just a girl in Hagersfield, they entered and exited the white world always by the back door, and usually at night. The exception to this was the Darling sisters, two maiden ladies who occupied a huge antebellum mansion on the outskirts of Hagersfield, and who kept a coloured butler from Jamaica with very fine manners and an earnest grasp of the King's English. The Darling sisters didn't seem to mind this coloured man to-ing and fro-ing on their property and were reported to often take their meals at the same table with him!

Mrs. Mellicant's husband is dead, and she has been a widow for fifteen years. They had no children — Mr. Mellicant's essential person being even too desiccated for that — so she is all alone in the world now, with nothing but her dead husband's business and his illustrious reputation for company. Mr. Mellicant has provided very well for her, much more than she ever expected, and she may, if she wishes, live out her remaining years in much the same comfort that she has always enjoyed. There is even a little for a modest holiday each year, should she choose to take it: to Atlantic City or Virginia Beach, perhaps with other ladies of her age and station. With Mr. Mellicant's demise, an entire universe of possibilities immediately yawned before her, and nowadays an unaccustomed liberty beats a thin pulse underneath her skin. She might go anywhere, do anything; she might behave as though she were a girl again. The idea of going back to Hagersfield does not occur to her. She takes the dead man's ledgers and goes into his study with them, examining them greedily, poring over them like Scripture.

And then, like Scripture, it smacks her dead between the eyes: Moses Shank. She feels a hot prickle of shame at the back of her neck, and tears find their way to her eyelashes, for Moses Shank is one of the richest men in Baltimore, a textile manufacturer, a coloured man. Entire pages are devoted to the finances of Moses Shank, here are his accounts. Here is evidence that Moses Shank's money has supported Mrs. Mellicant for all these years and is even now supporting her. The realization bursts upon her like a cold tide: she belongs to Moses Shank.

She can no longer face society, she thinks. Perhaps everyone except Mrs. Mellicant has always known the stippled underside of this secret; perhaps everyone is sneering at her in the street, whispering behind their hands. She is no longer Mrs. Mellicant, or even Mellicant's widow, but the concubine of Moses Shank.

And so her pew in the Presbyterian Church is empty, Sunday after Sunday, and she no longer goes to the Knitting Circle. Her soul, unnourished, flounders on the bedrock of her perceptions: she is living on coloured money, existing on the charity of a man whose boots she would not bend to wipe. She cannot leave her house, the house paid for by coloured money, purchased by the dark and evil Moses Shank. She wanders frantically from window to window, imagining a tide of coloured men marching up the sidewalk, coming to claim the house, the furnishings, and her. At last she steels her nerve and calls a locksmith, a white man from Kentucky, who fits every door and window with a complicated system of iron bars and steel deadbolts. When he goes away, she seals herself inside, satisfied that Moses Shank can never reach her.

Here is Mrs. Mellicant: a prisoner, and glad of it.

Vera Willoughby

Vera Willoughby is the oldest daughter, but there is one other girl, her sister Emily. Vera is a good girl — I can see this by her photograph — and she has always helped out in whatever way she can. She has volunteered on Church committees: serving tea, bundling boxes full of old clothes for the poor, baking shortbread cookies to take to shut-ins in the icy months of winter. She is everything a daughter ought to be, and in that, she is utterly unlike me, but the idea of this does not make me glad. I can look at her clean-scrubbed, tentatively smiling face and see the goodness shining out of her, and I wish that I had that kind of spiritual purity. Perhaps if I had her self-sacrificing impulse, then I might not be in the state I am. I might have managed to — no, that is too large a leap for anyone to make, especially me, and there are some things better left unsaid.

I wonder why it never seems to snow here. I'm looking out my window at the naked November trees and wondering what he is doing, all the way up there in Newfoundland. There will be snow there now, snow upon the naked trees, and snow scattered everywhere about the yard, drifted underneath the wheels of our new car, the car we bought just before he dumped me for some nurse he'd met, some hard-faced woman with a gigantic pigeon bosom and bright, brittle laughter. She is the kind of woman who wears high-heeled pumps with blue jeans, who has a rose tattooed upon her buttocks, who tries to dress like someone younger than she is. (She's forty.) Vera Willoughby would not approve of her at all, and I am obscurely glad.

I think Vera must have some sort of little job, the kind of job that women had in those days and she probably rides the bus to work, (despite sitting on a bumper of a car in this photo) waiting patiently in line with all the others at the curb in front of some neighbour's house. She knows enough not to sit beside a gentleman — for men contaminate by their very nearness! — but neither will she sit beside a child, or a girl of her own age. Vera Willoughby will always choose a seat (if there be one available) beside an older lady, someone who reminds her of her mother. Vera is such a good daughter! Her mother has given her to understand, as well, that young ladies from good homes must never work of necessity — but only as a means to gain experience of the world, which will then be paid out slowly, in metered doses, to whatever children God sees fit to bless her with. Vera will work as a means of amusement, then, until her parents grow too old to live alone, and then she will devote herself to their care and feeding. If Vera finds this a less than savoury prospect, I can see no evidence of it in her smooth and guileless stare. Perhaps she understands that girls like her are only ever fit for such things, according to the dictums of society. She looks to be intelligent (in the way that plain girls usually are), and I dare say she knows what waits for her beyond the threshold of her youth.

Vera, I think, is friendly and kind, but she is not attractive, unless you count warmth and a naturally good disposition in her favour. She has the kind of clean-cut features that are refreshing if not memorable; she is the kind of girl you would expect to see in advertisements for Chocolated Ex-Lax, discoursing upon the wonders of regular bowel movements and a sunny outlook. Her hair is frizzy, even though it is neither straight nor curly; she tries to keep it confined with a single barrette, placed like an iron girder at the top of her head, but to little effect. Her skin is uneven and pitted with tiny scars, the result of the terrible acne she had as a teenager. Her mother says that this was evidence of Vera's excessive intelligence, and it just goes to show that too much brain power in a girl only leads to bad ends. In her heart, Vera believes that her mother is right, but she cannot entirely reconcile her own outlook with her mother's views. Vera would like to be a scientist or a doctor — some exhilarating profession where her naturally sunny outlook would ensure a successful outcome. She wouldn't dare say this to her mother, for she knows that Mother would immediately launch into a shrieking fit, disavowing any knowledge of Vera as a child of hers. Mother would like for Vera to wither quietly at an office job for many years, paying for her own lipsticks and stockings and contributing her services as hostess at afternoon tea parties or sitting in the evenings with someone else's children. The chances of anything interesting ever happening to Vera are very slim, even though Vera is quite sweet and very accommodating. Her eyes are small, a nondescript shade of greenish brown, and her nose cannot be described as either dainty or feminine. She is the kind of girl you see cast as the sister or best friend of the heroine in old movies: always the bridesmaid, never the bride. Even her teeth will not stand up to scrutiny: they must be like the rest of her, small and dull coloured, unremarkable. Everything about her points to the fact that Vera is the quintessential good girl. Nevertheless, she lives a lush secret life of her own. Despite her little job, her attempt to gain "experience at life," she has always had dreams of being a scientist of some kind, and she reads library books about Madame Curie, as if she could obtain some of that woman's greatness through osmosis. Vera knows that, underneath her own unassuming surface, there is a seething volcano of secret desires, intellectual fantasies, great plans. Sometimes she thinks that unless this side of her is adequately vented, she will go mad. There is something there, deep inside, fastened underneath her rib cage, something that tugs at her in those moments when she is most alone.

Of course, she secretly hates her job, though it is an eminently respectable one for a young lady to have — perhaps she's some kind of receptionist or telephone girl. She especially hates her immediate supervisor, one Miss Pringle: an aged, withered spinster with stringy flesh and sensible shoes. Miss Pringle is probably about fifty, with iron-grey hair pulled back into a bun. Vera hates her because she recognizes something of herself in Miss Pringle, an unexplored potential for shrinkage that will only grow more powerful as she ages. Miss Pringle smells like mothballs, camphor and old cardboard, as though she had been stored for a long time in a dank cellar, deep under the earth. She wears iron-grey suits with grey shoes, and even her fingernails seem grey; her whole self seems about to merge into a single, unrelieved field of grey, washing out around the edges. Eventually she may disappear altogether. Vera has heard the tales — Vera knows that this is what happens to women who don't marry, who eschew the traditional, who choose their own paths. Miss Pringle is a vision of the future, a prophecy for Vera, who will ultimately take her place among the Pringles of the world and fade away. In Miss Pringle's presence, Vera often feels as though she were melting, dissolving; the attentions of Clive, the office boy (who breathes through his mouth noisily as he watches her) do not dispel this impression of impending decay.

Vera's life at home is overshadowed by her mother and her sister Emily, who is young, fragile and beautiful. Vera's mother has always been beautiful, and in her day she was courted by all the eligible young men and was much admired, for she comes from money, as they say. Her father was a steel man who made his fortune early in life; they kept a full complement of servants and even brought a butler from England, where he had served as some minor functionary in the house of the Earl of Suffolk. Thus, Vera's mother has always understood and appreciated the twin graces of wealth and beauty, and the outside world (with its greyness and its Miss Pringles) is not for her.

Emily is also beautiful and seems to be surrounded by a soft light, as though Heaven saw fit to spawn a little illumination on her. She always dresses in a billow of organdy: pink, yellow, seafoam green, champagne. She has a full rosebud mouth, perpetually moist, hesitating on the edge of being pursed, as though offering — or accepting — something. She has huge blue eyes, eyes that Vera, with her infinitely better personality, should have had, and is petite and well-made, where Vera is clunky. Emily is her mother's daughter in every respect, and has lots of beaus. Vera should hate Emily, but she doesn't — she doesn't have the energy. Besides, Vera is too nice to hate her sister.

And so Vera comes home one day to a scene where their mother is fitting a new dress on Emily, who is standing obediently and doe-eyed upon a chair. The dress is carnation pink, a froth of frilly stuff, like bubblegum. Their mother has a mouth full of pins and is down on her knees, labouring over this latest confection. "Emily is going out tonight," she says, when the last of the pins has been shed into the dress, "with Harry O'Malley's boy. You know Harry O'Malley, the judge? He's Irish, but it doesn't really matter, I suppose — Emily, stay still — they're quality, not the other kind of Irish, and I know for a *fact* that Harriet O'Malley is Temperance." Vera's mother immediately equates Irishness with drunkenness, as do most of her social set and generation.

"That's nice." Even though it's Saturday, Vera has worked all day in a dirty grey building downtown. Being a good girl, she always does as she's told, and if Miss Pringle needs her on a Saturday, then Vera will go, whether or not she had any other plans — but then, Vera never does. She is grimed with the dirt of the city, tired and sick, worn out from the ceaseless grind of answering the telephone to hordes of mannerless ruffians. Leaving the women alone with the dress, which seems to stand between them as some kind of icon, she goes upstairs to take a bath. She is glad of the rushing water, for it drowns out the beating in her head, the sound of Emily's giggles and her mother's coquettish replies. Vera sinks into the bath until only the tip of her nose is above the water and wonders what it would be like to drown.

Later, coming downstairs to get some toast and tea, she stumbles into the middle of her parents' inspection of Harry O'Malley the younger — Vera had forgotten he was coming (she spent her bath immersed in a dream of being the first woman on the moon) and is mortified that he should see her like this, in her slippers and shabby wrapper. But Harry is gracious, a tall, thin young man with spectacles and front teeth that project a bit too much. He isn't ugly, but he isn't the Adonis that her mother and Emily had made him out to be, either. "You must be Vera." He takes her hand in gentlemanly fashion, bowing stiffly from the waist as though they both were trapped in an eighteenth-century novel. "I am very pleased to meet you."

Vera cannot speak; having never been in a situation like this, she has no words for him. She always assumed that gentlemen would speak kindly to her sister, but never to her. The novels she smuggles into her bedroom invariably feature dark men who want to spirit girls away to forbidden English castles. *Wuthering Heights* is her favourite novel of all time, and during her lunch hour she dreams of wild Northern moors, of being surrounded by bleakness, an astringent for the soul. In reality, she is surrounded by a great sea of humanity, pressing her on all sides. Here, in Harry, she meets someone who, despite his beige hair and projecting teeth, is that shadow man embodied. And now she is shivering, the hand he holds in his is sweating, slippery. Her heart is throbbing in her throat, and bright lights revolve and burst before her eyes. When he takes his leave, her mother is indignant but waits until he and Emily have vanished down the walk. "Whatever possessed you to behave so?" she demands. "I want *Emily* to marry him — and then you can look after their children."

Vera turns and runs upstairs, locking her bedroom door behind her. She has no idea why she's crying. She doesn't want to know.

Emily and Harry seem to hit it off just fine, and they are the talk of Baltimore, are seen going hither and yon in Harry's car, stepping out in their finery to theatres and racy clubs, sometimes coming home just as the sun is up. Vera, miserable, avoids them both and agrees to work still more hours for the horrible Miss Pringle, if only to escape the oppression of her house. No one is surprised when Emily arrives home late one night, sporting a diamond on her finger. Harry is talking quietly to Mr. Willoughby in the study, where he was doubtless drinking whiskey behind the heavy leather doors, asking Mr. Willoughby to give him the hand of his daughter in marriage. Vera stands listening at the door, catches snatches of their conversation, feeling as though her skull were being crushed. She thinks about *Wuthering Heights*, about the brooding figure of Heathcliff — in her imagination, Harry could be Heathcliff.

She wants a man like that: a dangerous man who will ravish her with a thousand caresses. She watches Harry kissing Emily on the front steps, his hand reaching to squeeze her backside, crumpling the pink organdie dress. Vera spies on them, sees the way Emily's blonde head rests against Harry's manly shoulder. She wishes them nothing but the best, for Vera is a good girl.

Vera is a very good girl.

Desperado Deane

This girl's name is Deane, and she hates winter. She was ten when this picture was taken, and she's fourteen now. Look at her there, lolling on the beach with her hair tied up and her body soaking wet. Her mother was so insensible with pain at her birth that she thought the child was a boy; the doctor's exclamation of "Oh boy!" (a comment on Deane's size — she was a twelve-pound girl) mistakenly inferred that the child was male. Later, an *e* was added to Dean to try and feminize the name, but the damage was already done. Deane the Desperado, Desperado Deane — here she is, ten years old, kneeling in the wet sand like something washed up with the tide. Her skinny legs and non-existent breasts might belong to some androgynous sea creature, something without the luxury of a name. She's kneeling with her knees apart, daring the ocean to harass her. She knows she'll never be like other girls.

At ten Deane wore dungarees and went barefoot, hollered louder than the boys and swung on the topmost limbs of trees like a lemur. When a baseball knocked out two teeth, she exhibited her wound proudly. Rita, Deane's mother, would wring her hands and exclaim that Deane was abnormal and unnatural, that God had seen fit to punish Rita by sending her a boy in a girl's body, and what had Rita done to deserve that? She'd been a pious God-fearing woman all her life, except for the time she'd caught Leroy Trodden watching her get a bath through the window of her daddy's house and fetched up against his head with the iron frying pan.

Rita has tried to interest Deane in such womanly arts as sewing, needlepoint, and baking, but to no effect. At fourteen, Deane's monthly periods began, and Rita went limp with relief. The Lord had not abandoned her.

At age fourteen and two days, Deane discovered the Town Pump in Hagersfield, and the pool table, and Cletus Bigg, familiarly known as Big Cletus, who shoots the meanest game of pool from Hagersfield to Richmond and all points in between. Rita threw up her hands in black despair and prayed fervently for her daughter's soul, seeing as how Deane was intent on racing down the path to perdition.

Davis Trell, the manager of the Town Pump, isn't too thrilled with having a young girl hanging around his establishment, but as long as she minds her manners, doesn't drink or swear or chew, she can stay. And so Deane forsakes the usual entertainment of other girls her age and learns to shoot the sharpest game of pool in town. Pretty soon, she can play as good a game as any of the men, almost as good as Cletus Bigg. Her reputation at school begins to grow, and there is gossip all around Hagersfield; that she is the illegitimate daughter of Big Cletus, that she's gone and joined a gang of ruffians up Richmond way, that she's sold her soul to the devil.

Amelia Ditch is the unofficial leader of the girls in Deane's class: a pretty, petite pale blonde with great big eyes and a derriere shaped like an inverted Valentine heart. Amelia's father owns a clothing store in Hagersfield and several more just like it around the county. Amelia is what Rita would like Deane to be; she would settle for Deane and Amelia being as thick as thieves and prays to merciful Jesus to let it happen. Amelia approaches Deane at lunch one afternoon, as Deane is reading underneath the big elm tree behind the schoolhouse. She says, "We heard all about you. How you like to hang out at the Town Pump with all the degenerates." This is a new word Amelia has just discovered, and she likes the way it tastes inside her mouth. "You know what's going to happen to you, don't you? You'll end up selling yourself to some damn Yankee who'll fill you full of his Yankee spunk and get a bunch of Yankee brats on you."

Deane wonders how this transition has occurred: how she has gone from being invisible in Amelia's eyes to being an object of contempt. She knows Amelia is popular, and she knows Amelia is smart, but apart from these facts, it would be all the same if she and Amelia lived on different planets. She wonders what she might say in self-defence and realizes that there is no suitable response.

"Aren't you going to say anything?" Amelia demands. Several of the girls behind her titter nervously. "Maybe you already been with so many damn Yankees that you forgot your manners. Maybe you ain't even a girl at all!" And Amelia starts forward, catching the hem of Deane's skirt violently in her tiny fist. "Maybe you got something else in there!"

Deane slaps her hand away, mortified. She had been thinking about maybe going over to the Town Pump later on to play a few quick games against Big Cletus, listen to his stories about his great-granddaddy and the Civil War. She honestly doesn't understand that she has violated some unspoken social code, nor does she understand the ramifications. It does not occur to her that she will become an object of scorn and ridicule, quite apart from her mother's worry and fret.

The previous week, Deane remembers, her mother had a group of church ladies waiting at the house for her when she got out of school. Church ladies in their Sunday-go-to-meeting best, with straw hats and clean white gloves, bearing Bibles under their arms like weapons of war. She met Miss Delia White just inside the screen porch, staring down the dusty road as if waiting to spew forth prophecy. "Did Rita invite y'all here for afternoon coffee?" Deane is at the stage where she calls her mother Rita — this is one more indication of her declining moral sensibilities.

"We are here to pray for the salvation of your soul," Miss Delia tells her — and Deane realizes that Rita has gathered all of them for an impromptu prayer meeting. She intends to force some sort of holy intervention. She intends to manufacture Deane's repentance, even if it kills her.

Amelia is waiting for Deane at lunch the next day — Deane is sitting under the elm, eating a sandwich and thinking about her break shot, when Amelia and a group of boys appear, melting into life. They take her arms and legs, subdue her, make fat Charlie Evans sit on her chest, his piggy face close to her own, his fat thighs pinning her to the ground. There is screaming and laughter, and Deane struggles to get up, while probing hands tear at her clothes, examine her flesh. Someone reaches up under her skirt and rips away her panties, while someone else points, laughing, "Cunt, cunt!" The boys are shouting, laughing. "She's a girl!" Charlie Evans chases Amelia with the scraps of Deane's torn panties, and Amelia runs away, giggling and shrieking.

Deane wonders if this is the end of the world, and decides that it can't be, because she hears the school bell, shrilling out into the hot afternoon. She starts for home, wondering if Rita will have the house packed full of church ladies. She starts for home, but halfway there she changes her mind. She thinks about the church ladies and their wailing prayers, their saccharine worry for her soul.

Straightening her skirt and tucking in the fluttered tail ends of her blouse, she turns the other way and heads for the Town Pump and Cletus Bigg.

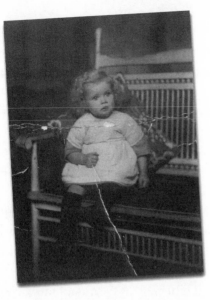

Bessie

Here is Bessie when she was three, small for her age and the apple of her momma's eye: plump, pretty, and blonde. Now Bessie is six and there isn't any picture of her: Daddy dropped their box Brownie down the well by accident, trying to take a picture of the trout he said was down there, and there's never any extra money for a new one. It only stands to reason that a child could be changed by more things besides time and weather, but Bessie hasn't changed, except maybe to get taller. Bessie's mother would always say to her, 'Give Momma some sugar, baby!" and Bessie would run to Momma and shower her with kisses.

Bessie's father used to work for a local sanitation company, somewhere in Hagersfield; Momma is plump and pretty like Bessie, but she walks with a limp, a result of polio in her childhood. The water was bad, back then, and children oughtn't to go swimming in it, but Momma did, and caught the polio bug. People in the town whisper that Fredrick Hamel only married Elizabeth because no one else would have her "with that leg of hers." Perhaps Freddie Hamel loved Elizabeth madly, leg and all, or perhaps he himself is no great prize and decided to take what he could get while it was still on offer. But Bessie gets teased at school these days by older girls who tell her that her mother is "nothin' but an old cripple woman!" and that she'll end her days immobilized in an iron lung. Bessie has never seen an iron lung, but she can imagine what it looks like, and inevitably pictures her mother imprisoned in a kind of cast-iron breastplate, like a figure from a Bible story. When the teasing becomes more vicious, Bessie runs to Momma to ask for the truth. She is young, but already she understands the value of truth, not merely those social truths we tell ourselves and others, so as to smooth the way — Bessie wants the *whole* truth, ripe and quivering on its stem. It's a funny thing about the truth, because you always think you want it. You think you're strong enough to take it, whatever it might be, but when it finally comes it hits you smack between the eyes like a fist. *I'm in love with someone else,* he said, right before he left me, and *she's not anyone you know*, which was untrue. He held the truth back from me and fed it to me in little pieces when he should have given me the whole thing, ripe and ready to fall into my hands.

"Who told you that, Sugar?" Momma is sitting in the backyard with a pan between her knees, breaking snap beans into it with a pleasant cracking sound, like many small bones being irrevocably broken. "Them big girls been tellin' you lies again?" It's all the same here in Hagersfield, where everybody knows everybody else's business, where neighbours lean across their fences or come up on your screen porch just to hear the news.

"They said you was gonna end up in a iron lung." Bessie watches Momma snapping beans; they ricochet crisply off the sides of the metal pan, and she enjoys the rhythm of it, like rain falling on the tin roof of their house.

"Darlin'" — Momma draws Bessie close — "It ain't true, what them girls say. I laid on my leg while I was sleeping one night, and it never straightened out — that's all!" And she lifts up her sensible cotton skirt to show Bessie the heavy metal brace that she must wear, clamped around her thigh. "I laid on it when I was sleepin'. It ain't nothin'."

But Bessie cannot erase the image of the brace, and when she gets into bed that night, she wonders if bad things happen when you go to sleep, and if this will happen to her, like it happened to Momma. What catastrophes are waiting for her in the darkened bedroom? What evil humours will seep into her presence, steal her breath? She gets under the covers carefully, making sure to lie on her back with her legs perfectly straight. She recites the Lord's Prayer until she falls asleep, hardly daring to breathe. The next day at school, Doreen and Betty come to her at recess, intent on pestering her as they always do. "There she is!" Doreen shrieks, and the small group of older girls come running, form a circle around Bessie so she can't move forward or backward. They are all bigger than she is, taller and more mature; their arms and legs seem impossibly long, their faces loom above her, their eyes and nostrils made enormous by the distance. They press in close to her, surrounding her like this, and they smell strange: like feet and underarms, like sour mash and a hint of barn. They are as poor and disadvantaged as she is, but Bessie can't possibly know this. All she knows is that they are surrounding her now, threatening and judging, intending to extract their pound of flesh — her flesh.

"I heard your Momma was a cripple." Judy Arle snaps her gum as quick as firecrackers, pressing bubbles through the gap in her front teeth. "I heard you're gonna be a cripple, just like your Momma, and a retard, too."

This is enormously funny to the girls, and they titter madly. Bessie watches all their faces, alert for any sign of kindness or softness, any possibility of reprieve. Perhaps one of them, an older girl, will say, *She's only a little kid. Leave her alone, you guys.* There is always that to hope for. "She laid on it when she was asleep," Bessie tells them. She is confident the truth will set her free. "And it got all crumped up like that. It ain't nobody's fault."

Sheila Martch (one of a pair of red-haired, freckle-faced twins, big and raw-boned and ugly) pokes a long, hard finger into Bessie's shoulder. "You're full of shit, Bessie Hamel. You're so full of shit that when you talk it flies out your mouth." This amuses them all; the others, too cowardly to swear on their own impetus, nevertheless enjoy hearing someone else do it. "I know how people get polio — that's what your Momma got, polio — they get it by swimmin' in dirty water. Your Momma was swimmin' in a *sewer*, and that's how come her leg's all twisted-like."

Bessie is upset by this — she cannot know that children don't possibly deduce such insights on their own, that children receive such knowledge from their elders. Bessie has seen the septic tank, when her Daddy had to dig it up and clean it out. He was toiling for ages, all through the night, digging it all up and carrying away great steaming buckets of nameless filth. She remembers, too, how the town council would go about with trucks in the early spring and clean the gutters, taking out huge shovelfuls of mucky black debris. She imagines her mother swimming in it, in her one-piece bathing suit with the frills, the one her father bought in Town, when they all went to Virginia Beach for holidays. In her imagination, now, Momma is swimming in this stuff, and being weighed down by her heavy brace: Bessie cannot shake the idea out of her mind. Her mother is covered in filth, and so Bessie must also share in this filth, by some obscure process of association. But the bell rings, ending recess, and the girls scatter, laughing at her behind their hands, secure in their secrets.

At supper that night, Bessie is so silent that her mother thinks she must be ill. "Are you ailin', child? Did you come down with something?" Momma reaches to brush Bessie's hair off her forehead, but Bessie pulls away from her, unable to look at Momma, unable to gaze into her eyes. When Daddy asks how school was, Bessie cannot answer him: the imagined filth has clogged her mouth and nostrils, stopped her speech.

"Bessie, you answer your Daddy!" Momma is alarmed and annoyed because Bessie has never behaved like this. "Your Daddy is talkin' to you!"

But Daddy has moved on to other topics, talking with his mouth half-full, talking on and on, "Russel Martch — just moved into town — owns a . . . what do they call it? A sanitation company." The Martches have two girls about Bessie's age: red-haired, freckle-faced, raw-boned girls with impossibly long arms and legs. What Bessie's father doesn't say is that he has recently approached Russel Martch for a job, since he's been let go from his old job when the business closed down. He gets dressed every day in a shirt and tie and takes a cup of coffee in the diner while he reads the want ads. To approach Russel Martch took great courage — he had to swallow his pride, as men do when they realize the scope of their mistakes or the position that they're in. Perhaps the March sisters were there the day he went to see their father; perhaps they know about his unemployment; perhaps they are only waiting to fling this fact of dissolution as far and fast as it will go.

They are waiting for Bessie the next morning, standing just inside the schoolyard, lounging near the gate in madras plaid dresses much too short for them. "It's Pissy Bessie!" They arrange themselves behind her, so that they are towering over her head, and follow her about the playground, no matter where she goes. "Your Daddy is a no-good scoundrel," one of them — Theresa — says, snapping her gum. "He come to our daddy looking for a job!" Indeed, Russel Martch had allowed himself the pleasure of laughing behind Fred Hamel's back, and in view of his daughters and his fashionable wife — too fashionable, Bessie's Momma would say later, for a woman whose husband shovelled other people's shit.

Bessie shrinks in upon herself, just as the teacher comes to rescue her. She feels like she's burning from the inside out as all these accusations swirl about her insides. The word *shame* might as well be marked there on her forehead, for all to see. She doesn't know what to do, how to behave, and she spends the rest of the day in a daze, pretending to pay attention to the lessons, feeling suspended in stopped time. She watches the other children in her class, but they all seem unreal to her, as if their faces were made of glass. She goes to the bathroom and gazes at herself in the mirror, trying to discern if there is anything behind her face: she doesn't look like she thinks she ought to look. She feels that her face would be charred and burned by now, that her head should be melting down into her neck, as though the insides of her eyes and nose, her forehead, had all grown too hot to last. She can't understand why she hasn't changed by now, why this awful truth has not crushed her. "This isn't real." And she smiles, gazing into the eyes of the girl in the mirror. An older girl comes out of a stall, passes by her on her way out of the bathroom, asks if Bessie said anything, but Bessie ignores her. Everything will be fine now

— she knows this. She can make anything be the way it was, just by thinking it so.

Her mother is pinning laundry on the line, a clean swath of white against the warm September sky. Her father is in his weekend clothes, on his hands and knees on the ground with a shovel, joking and laughing with Bessie's mother. A small part of Bessie wonders what they have to smile about, but this part of her is forced away by the rest, which insists upon this scene of normalcy. And indeed, when her parents move to greet her, it really is the same as always. She has succeeded in mastering an elusive magic. She knows how to elude the probing of her conscience. She has learned how to fool herself.

Jerry is a shopkeeper in the early 1930s, probably in Baltimore or one of its suburbs. He is outrageously young, but he graduated at the head of his class, and like those who achieve and possess early, he has a surprisingly keen sense of self. He is of Polish stock, but changed his name from Krzynski to Crane. His wife, Blanche, was a fashionable debutante, who married Jerry because she liked men with beards. Jerry shaved off his beard and Blanche, predictably, now likes him less. They have two children, Edward and Wilf, who are unremarkable in every way: Edward, the baby, is three, and still in short pants. Wilf is eleven, nearly twelve, and goes to public school for now, although Blanche thinks he'd be better off in a private school. Blanche doesn't like the influence of the public-school boys, with their loud voices and their ragged haircuts. Jerry says he can't afford it, but Blanche, married to him for this long, knows better: she's seen how well-stocked the shop is, selling everything from Epsom salts to stockings. The Great Depression is nearly two years old, but Jerry is still doing well. He still makes money, more than enough to go around.

Blanche will manipulate him on this point as one troubles a loose tooth with the tip of the tongue; eventually, Jerry will give in with no more than a token struggle.

Blanche is a woman of means — a private income came to her upon her marriage, a kind of matronage, a bequest from a great-great-aunt whom no one remembers and whom Blanche has never seen. "Remember where you came from," Blanche's mother told her, and Blanche has retained this: she is the daughter of an old Baltimore family, perhaps transmitted from Baltimore himself. She cannot afford to descend to commonness. Blanche's mother made much of their ties to Lord Baltimore, Cecilius Calvert, and the ancestors who helped to found St. Mary's City in the 1600s. Blanche must not forget their history.

Blanche has decided that she wants a family picture taken, to insert in the society pages of the prominent newspapers. It is a perfect opportunity to announce Wilfred's entrance into preparatory school, and Blanche wants everyone to know that they are still financially secure, immune from the fiduciary vagaries of the market. She especially wants to impress Mildred Baines, an old school friend with whom Blanche lunches every other Friday at the Calvert Room in Baltimore. Every other Friday, she and Mildred Baines meet there, and their choice of luncheon is always the same: a tiny salad with a dab of vinaigrette and the sumptuous flesh of Maryland blue crabs, taken from the Chesapeake. Mildred is always very firm on this point, and if Blanche should happen to arrive early, she knows to order this for Mildred and herself. There can be no variance: this menu is set in stone.

Mildred was always the beautiful one when they were girls, with great big, dark eyes and a cloud of wavy dark hair. Mildred, like Blanche, is of a prominent family, a family that helped to "build up Baltimore" — that is to say, had lots of money to begin with. Now, in the midst of the depression, their assets are still largely intact, and neither Blanche nor Mildred sees anything grotesque in this. Mildred has even gone one better: *she* has managed to marry a Congressman, one Hubert J. Walsh, he of the booming voice and walrus moustaches. Blanche has never quite forgiven her for this: it's one more insult to add to everything else she's had to endure with Mildred for all these years: Mildred's beauty, her charm and charisma, and now her social standing. Their wealth as girls was equal, but then Mildred married up, and Blanche married down. The truth is, Blanche doesn't even really *like* Mildred and each time, as she gets ready to go to their luncheon, she wonders why she doesn't just cancel. She has made a habit of stopping by the big mirror in the hall to look at herself as she fastens her hat into place. She sees the hard set of her mouth, her clenched jaw and wonders why she's angry. When did she become so angry? It has to do with Mildred, of course, but also with the fact that Jerry is a penny-pinching miser who spends hours each weekend crouched over a ledger, adding up figures with a strange, keen intensity. He is never satisfied with the results of his calculations, and must keep adding and subtracting, over and over; it makes Blanche's head ache and her jaw set as hard as granite.

Jerry resents her private income, her legacy, and Blanche has more than once made the mistake of offering to pay for things herself — to buy her own dresses, hats and gloves, or to pay for lunches at the Calvert Room with Mildred. This always sends Jerry into a rage, so that he spits when he talks, and beads of saliva gather in the corners of his mouth. He shouts at Blanche, "Your money is the only thing that you can think about!" Her money has unmanned him, has stolen his virility, and he accuses her of this and of other things, besides. She wants to turn Wilfred into a eunuch, Jerry says. She wants to turn him into a sissy-boy. It horrifies Blanche, who has never heard the word "eunuch" spoken aloud. While Jerry goes on with this tirade, she stands and stares at him, wondering how she could have married such a crude and vulgar man. Often, she is reduced to tears by the contemplation of his grossness, and then reminds herself that, unlike Mildred, she has married a common man who is a grocer, who has no breeding, who has no manners or sense of propriety. Jerry is a disaster in every way that matters to her. As for the sexual component of their marriage, that's something Blanche can't bring herself to think about, much less enjoy. She takes no pleasure in the natural congress of marriage, but allows Jerry to approach her because it is a woman's duty to cater to her husband's animal urges. Both of their sons were conceived in darkness, and her wedding night was only a few preliminary fumbles, some rooting about underneath her nightdress, and then a sudden sharp pain. She understood then, as now, that this would be expected of her with some regularity for as long as they were married, which would be forever. There is no escaping Jerry and his groceteria, Jerry and his elemental grossness. Even when he is dressed up in collar and tie, as he is on this picture, Jerry is still raw and somehow underdone, as though Whoever was responsible for his ultimate condition had removed him from the proving flames an hour too soon.

In the end, Blanche decides she will meet Mildred for their luncheon, as she has done so many times before. She is grumbling all the way there, because *she* must take the streetcar instead of driving. Mildred drives herself in a new automobile that her husband gave her for her birthday: another reason Blanche hates her. Blanche can't wear her diamonds or buy a car of her own, for such displays would inevitably enrage Jerry, remind him of all the things he has not provided. Blanche can afford to purchase an automobile for herself, but is prevented by the memory of Jerry's last tirade, and the promise of future rages. So Blanche has to ride the streetcar and be disgusted by the low, mean class of people that she's forced to associate with on these twice-monthly rides. She resents Mildred, too, for this, and tells herself it is all Mildred's fault. If Mildred did not exist, then Blanche would not have to endure this: Jerry and his greed, the streetcar ride, the inevitable lunch of crabs culled from the Chesapeake. Blanche doesn't even like crabs.

But here is Mildred, looking splendid as usual, and here is Blanche, feeling dowdy and ill-dressed in her presence. Mildred's gloves are of a particular shade of dove-grey, to match her particular, dove-grey suit; Blanche's gloves are old, and so tight that her fingers have the appearance of sausages. She removes the gloves as quickly as possible, hides them in her purse. There is a small cut near her top of the right index finger — a kitchen accident when Blanche was cutting up carrots for stew. Jerry will not allow her to employ a cook or even a maid, although Blanche is grossly overworked and required to take on the meanest of menial duties. She cannot avoid cleaning the toilets and emptying the slop water over the back stoop. She knows that such things diminish her; she knows that they are not required of Mildred, who has a cook, at any rate, and probably several maids.

Blanche isn't even listening to what Mildred is saying, she is so concerned with her own thoughts. She is wondering how she will convince Jerry to let her send Wilf to private school. She wonders if Edward will grow up to be like his father. She is contemplating the cut on her index finger and wondering how she can possibly hide it from Mildred, who has always had eyes like a chicken hawk. But now Mildred is saying something in an insistent tone — so insistent that Blanche is forced to break her reverie and pay attention. She glances up at her friend, momentarily dazzled by the sparkling diamond brooch on the lapel of Mildred's particular grey suit. Mildred is wearing a matching ring, with a huge, pear-shaped diamond set in gold. The diamond is so large that it threatens to swallow her knuckle. Blanche feels as though something is caught in her throat, something roughly the size and shape of that diamond ring. Every petty jealousy she's ever harboured against Mildred is focussed on that ring as it captures the light and throws it back again, a thousand glistening, icy darts. Now Mildred is showing Blanche some family pictures they had taken a few weeks before: Mildred, lovely, in a white gown with a froth of lace at her throat, and her husband looking prosperous in a good suit, his broad, open face beaming in an expression of goodwill. Their two daughters are miniature replicas of Mildred, petite and dark-haired, with her huge, soul-searching eyes. In contrast, Blanche's boys have always looked slightly stupid, as though they had been surprised in some curiously repugnant personal act. Jerry's low brow and blank expression depict a man who is too easily satisfied, who never looks beyond himself, who could never beam goodwill from a broad and open face.

It's wholly unnatural to have the kind of good fortune that Mildred displays; it is a clear indication, Blanche feels, of their endless struggle to best one another, all through their long association. To manifest such wealth is vulgar, and now Blanche is obscurely glad that she has refrained from it. As they examine the shared photographs, she thinks that perhaps Mildred has found some dark means by which to gather these things to her — some kind of witchcraft, a summoning. There is an intimation of evil in the banal faces of Mildred's family, and she can't take her eyes from the photographs of Mildred's broad and stalwart husband, the sinister dark eyes of the daughters. Blanche is cold all over, as though someone were pouring icy water down her back; she leaves the table abruptly, murmuring some excuse about feeling unwell.

"Why, Blanche —" Mildred half rises from her chair, then sinks back down again, one hand against her throat, fluttering in a gesture of surprise. She watches Blanche disappear into the mass of potted palms, the gleaming gold backs of the luncheon chairs, and finally, the smoky, liver-coloured air.

The inevitable luncheon date looms ahead of Blanche two weeks later, and for several days she wanders the rooms of her house in a state of cold panic, wringing her hands. She cannot escape the images, sinister and profane, that rise into her consciousness: Mildred and her evil husband, and their per-nicious children. Finally, with a supreme effort of will, she takes Mildred's calling card out of her desk and slowly rips it into many tiny fragments. She feels terrified as she does this, as if she is committing a mortal sin. She can hear Jerry, muttering over his accounts in the study, the smell of his cigar drifting upwards to her nostrils, bitter and acrid as brimstone. Her heart beats in her throat and she feels quite faint as she tosses the pieces of card into the trash.

Then she feels strong. She walks away, calling to her children who have just come home from school.

Paddy and Michael

What sort of a story can I tell you about Paddy and Michael Murphy? And where should I begin — or, more to the point, which of their stories should I tell? They are St. John's Roman Catholic boys, as hard as Newfoundland granite, brought up with the least of everything. Paddy is the younger of the two, and in the picture he looks like a monkey, smiling with a positively simian aspect, his small, triangular face turned eagerly towards the camera. His fists are clenched as if he has something to prove. He's pugnacious by nature, this much I can readily tell, and he will certainly endure a great many schoolyard fights before he grows to manhood. He will be a scrappy fighter, small and wiry, and those who are too large for him to fight, he'll run away from. He has an excellent instinct for self-preservation.

Michael is his brother, and they both go to the same Roman Catholic school, the sort of establishment or edifice that at once speaks the language of the oppressor and the oppressed. Paddy enjoys school because it brings with it a daily assortment of scintillating fights. Michael is not like his brother: Michael would never raise a hand in anger. Even when Paddy beats him mercilessly, Michael is silent except for a slight smile that plays about his lips and then is gone. Michael wants to be a priest and has decided that patient forbearance in the face of adversity is the right way to handle the sorts of assaults that Paddy launches. Michael has a set of rosary beads that Father O'Brien gave him at Lent, and he wears it inside his clothes, never taking it off, not even when he bathes. At night, the beads press an imprint into the fish-pale flesh of his torso, but he accepts this as necessary penance. Michael is gentle where Paddy is rough, wise where Paddy is foolish, quiet where Paddy is loud. One would surmise that, if good things were to happen to either of these boys, then Michael would be the lucky one. It makes sense, after all. It's only fair.

So Michael grows up and becomes a priest, and Paddy gets a job in a hospital, cleaning up after operations. He doesn't mind the human body and all its gory spillage because it's not so different from the schoolyard fights, when he pummelled Billy Francis' nose into a bloody pulp, all those years ago.

Michael is a good priest, dedicated to his parish as only one who truly believes can be. For Michael, the hush and glow of the holy sacrament is mystical, astonishing. The organ sounds of the late-night masses trouble him, however, and he wonders if there is a flaw in his faith somewhere. He resolves to spend more time on his knees, more time reciting his prayers. When he retires to his little room at night (it is a *little* room because Michael feels more and more that excess is an affront to righteousness) he stays on his knees until the sun comes up.

But it doesn't help. After a while, the music and the organ sounds follow him; he can't escape the noise. During Mass one Sunday morning, he hears the sound of God's own voice exhorting him to proclaim the Holy Trinity. He goes up and down the pews, gazing deep into his congregation's eyes with an attitude of lunacy. Shortly after this, one of the deacons places a call to Paddy, who is at work, in the act of sweeping spattered bits of bone off the operating room floor. Paddy won't be off work for another hour and a half, but he will come as soon as he can, he says. He hasn't seen Michael for ages. Being a non-believer, Paddy never goes to church, and he isn't likely to meet Michael in a common social setting. While Michael is praying on his knees, Paddy is downing pints of Harp or Smithwick's at the pub.

When Paddy arrives, Michael has commanded the organ noises to be silent. He offers Paddy a cup of tea and pours for them both. Michael keeps no housekeeper, not wanting to expose himself to the temptations of the flesh. Besides, another person in close proximity would doubtless find it odd to see Michael on his knees all day and half the night. Whatever small measure of housekeeping needs to be done, Michael will do it himself. That's the best way to handle things, he thinks, and this is what the organ sounds have told him. This he knows to be the truth. He talks to Paddy about general things but watches his brother with wariness, as though Paddy might suddenly spring an unexpected question.

Paddy isn't there the day Michael throws all his personal belongings out the window. Nor is Paddy around when Michael takes a paintbrush and paints the windows of the rectory black, shutting out all natural light. The parish council is called in, and they debate far into the night: *What shall we do about Father Murphy?* And still the organ tones roll on, drowning everything. At last, Michael climbs up onto the roof of the church one chilly February night, shivering and stark naked. He is alone as he stands there, gazing heavenward, and he is alone as he slips down the icy shingles to his death. He leaves his rosary beads to Paddy, but in his will there is no word about the organ sounds, the choir, or the voice of God.

My Pretty Peggy

Here is Peggy, sitting on a toy horse, holding a toy bow and a quiver of arrows. Peggy might be playing cowboy, except she's wearing a tunic and tights, and she looks as if someone dressed her in these clothes against her will. She has the saddest and most lovely face that I have ever seen on a child, and an expression of melancholy, the intimation of knowledge beyond her years. It's tempting to ascribe motive to this expression, to look for cause, but perhaps she's merely serious, a child with an ancient soul. I've found this photo in the box of things I brought with me, but I don't know who the child is, or was. Perhaps she's an aunt I've never met, or an older sister who somehow vanished before I was born. Perhaps she's me, the way I ought to have been.

Peggy's parents, expatriate Newfoundlanders, are moving back home after an absence of several long years. The time has been an exile of sorts in northern Ontario, with no one around who knows them, with no one around who cares when they fight, or when Peggy's mother cries for days on end. No one knows why Peggy's mother cries — certainly not Peggy and certainly not her mother. The fits of weeping come upon her suddenly, without provocation or cause, and she wanders from room to room in their rented house, staring out of windows at the parched and flattened, nickel-blasted landscape. It's because of the crying that Peggy's father and her Uncle Max have decided the time has come to leave Sudbury. They talk about their vanished island as though it were the promised land; they reminisce at the supper table, sitting amongst empty Kentucky Fried Chicken buckets, crunching bones with the alacrity of barbarians.

Peggy's mother, because of the constant weeping, is unable to cook, and when Peggy's father comes home from the nickel mine, he brings buckets of chicken, milkshakes and pizza, stubby brown bottles of beer. Sometimes they play Crazy Eights after supper, while Peggy's mother gathers up the remnants and feeds them to the cat — the shelter cat that will run away some morning soon and end up flat and bloodied on LaSalle Boulevard. Peggy remembers being taken to the SPCA shelter some Saturdays ago. She remembers being taken by the hand and led among the cages, gazing into the eyes of the abandoned animals. She finally chooses a black and white cat with luminous golden eyes. When they get home, the cat disappears behind the davenport and does not come out for a week, except late at night, when it leaves trails of excrement and puddles of urine throughout the house. Peggy's father, disappearing into the nickel mine each morning, curses the cat until Peggy's mother cries again.

The days seem flat and endless, broken by meals and trips to the bathroom, an attempt to make cat toys out of string and empty toilet paper rolls. The toilet paper is pink, to match the black-and-pink bathroom walls, and the tub is also pink. Peggy imagines that the water in the tub is like the water they will all be crossing very soon, when they go to Newfoundland to see her grandmother. But this holds no fascination, because Peggy can't or doesn't remember what this vanished island is about, does not remember her grandmother or the white clapboard house set down among the endless tributary hills. She has only ever known this northern Ontario town, the rumble of trucks on LaSalle Boulevard, the chunk of nickel that her father brought home, dark and glistening, poisonous-looking. She only knows the familiar hallways of this rented house, the roar of traffic, the stench of sulphur from the smelter. In later years, she won't remember how she got from this grey Ontario town to the ferry terminal at North Sydney — she will only remember the broad swath of cold blue ocean, rising and falling under the bow of the boat.

It's raining when they arrive, and somewhere during the voyage Peggy has turned five. The rain is a steady, soaking drizzle, falling relentlessly. It seems to take a very long time to reach her grandmother's house. She has never seen so many green trees, so much vegetation. When she steps out of the car, she feels the island rise to her, a presence pushing through the mist. It rushes to her with the force and magnitude of a November gale, pours through her. She knows she will never leave this place. She knows that this place owns her. She will accurately divine its melancholy and its joy.

Moira Doone

Moira Doone just got out of the San, and she's glad to be home. Here she is, in the field near her brother's house on Logan's Hill in Guernsey, the tiny Newfoundland fishing village where she was born. Her brother's name is Liam, and for most of his life he's worked down through the country in the lumber woods cooking for the men, for Liam had his own brush with tuberculosis and isn't as strong as he used to be, nor as he'd like to be. He built his house himself with his own two hands, hauling wood with the dogsled in the winter, hauling it out from deep in the back country where the lynxes are, where there might be bears. In the summertime, he hauled the wood again, this time on a wagon that old Maisie, Liam's mare, pulled with patient, plodding steps. Jim Dyke sawed and planed the boards in his mill, and when Liam had enough for a house, he set to work. This was while Moira was still in the San with a particularly virulent TB of the spine and not expected to live — but Liam believed that his sister would get well again, and so he set about making her a place that she could come home to. He made her a house of her very own, set high upon the hill, for Liam loved his sister without reservation.

Spring has just broken on the day that Moira is released from the San, and when Liam brings her home to the Hill, the winds are warm, and the fresh-turned earth smells sweet and rich and moist. The Hill is already green, a deep and glistening green, and the new leaves are already crowning at the tips of branches. The silvery alders clack their limbs together at either side of the road leading to the new house, which is white, clapboarded. Liam has asked Bessie, who lives on the lower slope of the Hill, if she would sew curtains, and she has done so, but there wasn't enough fabric in the shop to make matching sets, so Bessie has dressed each window individually.

Liam has not told Moira about the house, has deliberately kept the secret all this time. Even on the long drive out from town, he has talked of many things: the new lambs that wait for Moira's touch, up in the stable, and the bed of daffodils and hyacinths that he has planted near the kitchen's crisp half-door. He nearly gives himself away with this, but perhaps Moira thinks he's talking of the old house down in the valley, whose timbers are rotted with moisture. He wants her to be surprised and joyful, and he wants her to live here in this house with him, a brother and his adored older sister, until their days are ended. He knows that no one will ever marry him, despite his rich dark hair, his pale green eyes. Tuberculosis has left his spine deformed, one shoulder higher than the other, and although he knows that he is strong and only twenty-five, no woman will take him as a husband. No woman will ever think of him that way — and besides, he is shockingly illiterate, having put to sea at twelve, when Da was still alive, and then going to the lumber woods at seventeen. He knows what it is to work hard, but he cannot read or write and only learned the tracing of his own signature by rote. The contents of it, that pained and mangled alphabet, mean nothing to him. He signs cheques and greeting cards, letters and pictures with his tortured signature, which is better, after all, than an X. He is savage in a lot of other ways as well, given to fits of self-hatred. He spends long hours alone in the stable, caring for the animals and whittling on a piece of wood. He wants to think his own thoughts, which move as fast as lightning. He wonders if his sister loves him.

Liam waits until the taxi turns the final bend in the road. Moira has her head turned, is gazing out the window at the surrounding greenness of the hills, lost in her own musings. Far away, down in the valley, a line of laundry twists and dances in the breeze: men's trousers, skirts, a woman's apron, baby clothes. Moira's hair is thick and dark like her brother's, but where his stands up in tufts and wispy feathers, hers flows around her head, as billowy as a confined cloud. She has the same pale green eyes, but her habitual expression is rather closed, secretive. Liam is never really sure whether he can trust her.

He waits for her to see the house, to realize that this is where the taxi is going. He is excited but fearful: what if she doesn't want a house, or has no intention of living here with him? He decides that he won't think of such things. He is tugging at her sleeve to make her turn around; he is desperate for her to see it, to recognize the homage he has made. She is still gazing back at the line of laundry in the valley, flapping in the breeze.

"Moira, we're home. This is our house — your house. I

built it for you, all by myself I built it, just for you, so you could have a home, so we could have a house." His words tumble over one another in his haste; his pale green eyes are wet with tears that he will not let fall. Everything in him strains along two divided planes of longing: Moira and the house.

She is in a partial body cast that encloses her from chest to hip. She must walk leaning on two canes, and both Liam and the taxi driver have to lift her up out of the car. The weight of the cast drowns her slight body between them, and for a moment she hangs motionless, supported on one side by the burly taxi man and on the other by her brother's twisted shoulder. Moira's eyes are closed as she leans against the car, waiting while her brother rummages amongst the baggage for her canes. Her eyes are closed, and she can hear the seagulls, smell the softness of the April winds. *Home,* she thinks, *I'm home*. And then the spell is broken and Liam is handing her inside the house, and the taxi disappears down the hill. She is alone up here with her brother. She is all alone with Liam.

Moira knows what Liam is thinking, knows that he is waiting most of all for her reaction to his labour, to the shrine that he has made for her. She ought to be delighted, and she is surprised, but not in the way Liam would like her to be. There are things she needs to tell him, but first she lets him lead her through the house, as through a labyrinth. He has made the rooms spacious, the doorways wide enough for Moira and her canes to pass unhindered. He has brought her bed up from the old house in the valley and set it next to a sunny window. A handmade quilt that she has never seen before is pulled up to cover the sheets, and Moira's white cotton nightdress is laid lovingly across the pillows. There is a clutch of wildflowers in a drinking glass upon the nightstand:

ox-eyes and goldenrod, cow flowers and wild irises, blushed a deep and bloody purple.

The windows of the rooms look out upon the surrounding greenness, the blue wash of the sea beyond. It is a house with its face turned outward, seeking contact, a house that is forever hopeful, forever eager. She finds her voice long enough to tell her brother, "Thank you." Then she professes weariness, closes her door on him, and lies down on the bed that he has brought to her in the house that he has made. He is halfway to the stable when she realizes that she has not told him. She has not told him anything.

He is trying not to think of Moira as he goes up the hill to where the stable is, equidistant to both the house and the ancient cellar, half-buried in the ground. Liam doesn't know who made the cellar or where it came from. Before he ever built his house — Moira's house — the cellar was there. He shored up the crumbling stone roof and laid fresh sods over the naked places in its grassy skin. When he harvests the modest portion of vegetables that he has planted, later in the fall, he will store them here, safe from frost and winter.

The stable is his sacred enclave, the place he goes for solace, to whittle on a piece of wood. For some months now, while Maisie and the sheep watch silently, he has been whittling a series of small figures which he has painstakingly painted, laying marks of recognition down upon their dull wooden faces, layer by layer. He has made several sets of these, which he arranges in tableaux: the figure of the man, in navy dungarees and tartan shirt, is waited on at table by the woman with her cloud of flying dark hair and faded cotton dress. Each tableau features a similar domestic scene, each quite harmless, but the detail with which he has endowed the faces of the two is a little frightening. Liam cries as he whittles the newest pair, which will depict him chopping wood outside, while Moira, standing at the kitchen's half-door, is truncated at the waist as though her body were severed in two. It will be the way it used to be, before Moira went away, before her spine got bad and she coughed up blood. They will sit before the fire on long winter nights like they used to do, and Moira will read aloud to him from his favourite books: Jonathan Swift or Jane Austen or the poems of John Keats. *Thou still unravished bride of quietness* . . . Moira has always been the quiet one, receptive and smooth as a mythic Grecian urn. Moira was always the smart one, the one everyone thought would do so well out in the world, while it was expected that Liam would want to stay close to home. He would have gone anywhere with her, done anything for her, and he still would. He remembers her as she was on long-ago summer afternoons, racing him through the meadow at the foot of the hill or plucking wildflowers to weave into a crown for his dark head. "Thank God he got his sister to keep an eye out for him," people often said, tapping at their temples as they did so. "Thank God one of them got the brains."

He is thinking about his sister, about the absoluteness of the silence in her eyes. He cannot understand what she is thinking about, nor why she isn't thinking about him. He would like to splinter the house he has made, take his axe to it and break it up into matchsticks, leave it to fly away on the wind. He knows that he exists in silence now, in the spaces between words. Moira has always made for him a jewelled net of language, a shared history of lifelong plans and stories, the mesh that forever binds him to her. He feels that he is slipping through the spaces. He feels as though his flesh will fall on nettles, that these nettles will spear him through the heart.

"Liam?" Moira moves uneasily up the lane, swinging her heavy cast between her canes. She has not seen her brother since last night, and when she checked the stable a moment ago, he wasn't there. She knows she must explain. She knows that he is thinking about the nets, the meshes and the holes. "Liam."

He is here, behind the house, chopping wood for kindling. The day is warm for so early in the spring, and he is stripped to the waist. Sweat glistens on his skin, his hairless chest. His misshapen shoulder seems always in the act of raising itself. At such a narrow distance, Moira can see the bend in his spine, the heinous defect. "Here you are," she says, unnecessarily.

Liam chops with a particular cadence, ignoring her for several long moments. He stops, drinks water from a dipper by his side, regarding his sister with quiet suspicion.

"I have to talk to you." She sits down on one of the two stumps that Liam uses for chopping blocks, lays her canes to one side. The winds are warm, delicious, and she considers carefully what she is about to say. She knows how sensitive he is, knows that he cannot bear infidelity or rejection. "I'm going to have a baby."

This falls into a silence more profound than any she has ever heard. She and Liam are stilled in this tableau, like his whittled wooden figures. The warm winds lift the hem of her dress, toy with it, drop it back around her knees again. Liam is staring at her, and his eyes are the green of the surrounding hills. When he finally speaks, it is to utter just one word. "Whose?"

The axe is lying useless in his hand, although he knows that he could raise it quickly, more quickly than anyone might think.

"A doctor at the San. His name is Reg. He's English, from Somerset. He's going to marry me, Liam. He wants to take me to England, to live there."

But her brother is turning away, as if in slow motion, his body bending to retrieve the axe, his tortured shoulder asserting itself, a shape like a wedge.

"He's going to marry me, Liam, so there's no need to worry —"

The axe swings through an arc, the ancient blade flashing silver in the sunlight. As he brings it down, Liam feels nothing, and when it bites into his wrist, severing the hand, he still feels nothing. He staggers towards Moira, who struggles to get up, the heavy cast holding her immobile, robbing her of motion. The heel of her shoe catches on some unseen obstacle, and she goes over onto her back, falling with a sickening crunch that all but shatters the cast.

He fills her field of view, and she can see nothing but his bloody stump, pulsing its life out onto her. The house is silent behind them, peering at them both with guileless eyes. *You can't leave me,* it says. *You can never leave me.*

The Divining

Here is a picture of Horace and Jack, taken just before Jack died. Jack is on the left, dressed in a suit and tie, as if he's going to church or to a funeral. Even his shoes are shiny. He looks like an old picture of some obscure, vanished writer from another age — an almost-Joyce, a not-quite Fitzgerald. It's amazing that Jack should be with Horace in this picture, both of them sitting in the middle of the woods, when Jack clearly has business elsewhere. Jack is a water witch, a diviner, and he does his work with a willow branch, or sometimes with an alder switch if it's all that he can find. He always dresses up for these occasions, as if he were called upon to do God's work, and this is why he's wearing his Sunday best. He has to go down into the valley, where you think there'd be lots of water, and find a well for Freddie Davis and his wife. Sheila Davis is in the family way, expecting their fourth, and Freddie just built a new house where Liam and Moira Doone used to live years ago, before Liam built that new house up on the hill, and Moira married her doctor and went overseas. The Doones' old house had stood there for as long as anyone could remember, but the timbers were all rotten on account of the continual falling damp. Freddie could have built anywhere he liked, but Sheila wanted to live in the valley, and so they tore down the Doones' house. This was just after Moira left, just after Liam set fire to the new house and then drowned himself in Butler's Pond. When Cec Peddle found him, Liam had a rope around his neck with a rock tied to it.

Jack always dresses up whenever he goes to witch a well — he and Horace have been friends ever since they were boys, ever since Jack fished Horace out of the harbour when he fell off the wharf. It's always been that way with Jack and Horace, just as it has been with Jack and water: a certain sensitivity of touch, an assuredness. Horace wishes he had Jack's particular gift, but he doesn't. Horace makes nets at Harry Bishop's twine loft, up the road a ways. From time to time, he has crafted small tourist items: two children in a boat hauling a miniature grapnel aboard; a housewife in a carefully painted-on apron, making fish on a pebbled beach, shrunken to a fraction of its actual size. Horace doesn't make the figures anymore — not after what happened to Liam Doone — but confines himself mainly to rough-hewn dories, painted in improbable shades. He doesn't mind spending his days knitting twine, but sometimes, when he really thinks about it, he's a little jealous of Jack, would like to have Jack's talent. Horace's gifts are fine enough, but he wishes he could do the fantastical thing that Jack does, create miracles out of the dry and dusty ground.

Jack comes to see Horace at the twine loft, just as he's getting ready to go and witch for Freddie. Horace is knitting with concentration, the twine needle flying in and out of the holes. Gradually, the net takes shape at his feet, growing in size, spreading out beyond him to touch the walls of the twine loft. It's a cold morning in March, with spring many, many weeks away, and Jack is dressed up as usual, but wearing a dark overcoat which gives him the air of an undertaker. He steps inside the closed door and stands motionless, his nostrils flaring slightly as he scents the ever-present smell of fish that seems to emanate from the walls, oozing out of the rough-hewn boards.

"Whatta ya at?" Horace asks. This is a formality only — he knows what Jack is at, knows where Jack is going. The odd thing is, in all the years they have known one another, Horace has never gone along to watch this thing that Jack does. He tries to remember if Jack has ever invited him, but he can't seem to recall if Jack has. Although he knows exactly how it's done, he has never seen Jack do it, and he would like to, but he will never be brazen enough to ask. If he is to be invited, Jack must invite him, must indicate by the proper gestures that Horace is welcome.

"Goin' down to Freddie's the once." Jack is smoking a cigarette, has smoked it almost to the butt, and what remains of it protrudes from his face, rootlike. "He needs that well before Sheila's time is come."

"Yes, b'ye." The needle wafts between them, spinning twine; the net at Horace's feet grows larger, moves in tiny increments towards Jack, as if to snare him in its gaps and holes.

"Sure, why don't you come along?" Jack moves the cigarette stub to the other side of his mouth, the better to talk around it.

"Nah." Horace doesn't even pretend to think about it. "You go on, b'ye. I got work to do." He doesn't look at Jack, doesn't want him to see the jealousy in his eyes. He thinks it's unfair that he should have to stand here knitting twine when Jack can go down into the Doones' old valley and find water with nothing but an alder switch or a willow wand. "Mind you don't fall in, now." He says this with a cackle, knowing that Jack won't laugh, but needing to make the joke anyway. Horace makes this same joke every time Jack goes to witch a well — it's some sort of tradition between them, a custom that has grown out of their long association.

"I'll see ya later." Jack doesn't turn his back on Horace, but steps backwards out of the twine loft, successfully negotiating the single step (a concrete slab) without turning around. Only when he can no longer see Horace through the building's opened door does he turn, walk quickly away in the direction of the valley. He doesn't know that Horace is watching him through an aperture in the loft's ramshackle walls, that Horace tracks his progress as he has so often tracked the destructive path of a storm at sea. Horace cannot resist doing this, just as he cannot resist tapping the face of any barometer within his range. It's his way of finding out what will happen, of predicting the future through close observation of seemingly mundane details. Perhaps he doesn't really know — but whatever he knows, Horace is keeping it to himself. And so he stays there in the twine loft, while the March winds kick up a living storm outside, and hard pellets of grainy snow plummet from the sky, assaulting the spongy ground. He measures the hours by the imagined passage of the unseen sun across the sky. The net grows larger, foaming over itself, reaching to the doorway and beyond, and still Horace knits, the needle flying ever faster, seemingly without pause.

He lights the lamp at dusk and waits, gathering the fresh net up into his hands. He hears them coming: the sounds of men and horses cresting the hill, the sound of disembodied voices falling like a hammer blow upon the hushed casket of his soul. They have brought Jack with them: laid out dark and still and stark, his Sunday best creased and rotten with the filthy water, his cold-wrinkled hands crossed summarily upon his breast. What was he doing there anyway, and why did he choose to take the shortcut in the dark, and why did Freddie find him up in Butler's Pond, a stone around his neck?

Horace watches the cortège as it passes by, nods to the men as they mumble sombre greetings. The parade of men is struck silent by this event, and so is Jack's sister Rita, bringing up the rear. Heber Pryor's dog detaches itself from the funeral procession and moves to gaze at Horace, standing in the doorway of the twine loft, his hands full of the heavy warp and weft. The dog will not come near him, but stops some distance away, ears laid flat against its head, its wet coat glistening in the cruel twilight of early March. Heber passes the net back and forth between his hands and watches the procession vanish into the looming darkness.

The dog watches, growling in his throat, and moves back in line with the procession, disappearing with it over the hill.

A Suitable Woman

Elizabeth has been away at college, studying to be a veterinarian. She wants to live on the trackless barrens, somewhere far away from here, tending sheep and cattle, living in a cottage with stout walls and thick old windows, the kettle on the hob. She has come home for the weekend, long enough to visit with her mother and to pose for this photograph in the back yard of their family home in Harbour Grace. The grass has grown up in her absence; it is nearing the end of August now, time for Elizabeth to return to study. Before she boards the Sunday morning bus to university, she will change into a pair of her dead brother's overalls, don a pair of rubber goat boots, and mow the yard one final time. The push mower is old, and its rusty blades hack and stutter at the grass. But Elizabeth is stubborn, and besides, she likes the exercise. It will help her in the future, she thinks. It will strengthen her for what is to come.

Her mother, so glad that Elizabeth has been home, cannot bear to speak of her daughter's imminent departure. As the weekend winds itself into a warp and weft of things unsaid, she busies herself in the kitchen, preparing little cakes and loaves of bread for Elizabeth to take with her on the bus. She hurries from the counter to the cupboards, from the cupboards to the pantry, and from there to the oven's opened mouth. Tears drop into the dough as she kneads, her muscular arms squeezing, shaping the loaves, and she wipes her tears in the hem of her apron, while Elizabeth's mower cuts narrow paths in the surfeit of grass. Eventually, Elizabeth thinks, she will have to tell her mother. Eventually, there will have to be a reckoning, not unlike confession, where she will tell her mother everything. She has privately murmured over this decision all weekend, enumerating the reasons, and she has decided to tell her mother when they get to the bus. She will have to. She cannot bear the burden of the secret any longer. If she doesn't speak this truth out loud, then it will burst her frame wide open. She feels it pulsing underneath her breastbone, waiting.

Elizabeth's mother has something to tell as well — something that cannot wait, something that will not be put off, something that must be spoken. Many times she has tried to frame it in a letter to her daughter, addressed to the veterinary college, and many times she has laid the crumpled paper carefully among the oven's burning coals. It isn't speculation any longer: there is the doctor's evidence, the months of bloodied undergarments smelling curiously of yeast and rust, a melancholic bottom note of rot. This must be spoken. It cannot be allowed to lie between them, filling up their familiar spaces.

Elizabeth finishes the mowing and goes into the house, leaving her boots just outside the door. She is acutely conscious of the sentiments of trespass and rinses her hands at the garden tap. The margins of her fingernails are stained deep green, the blood of August. Soon, the stubble fields upon the hillsides will turn brown and dry, crackling in the watery sunlight. Summer will die quietly and quickly, a blown-out candle.

Their evening meal is simple: soup that her mother has made, slices cut from a fresh loaf of bread, some cheese. The daylight dies quickly behind the curtains; there is silence save for the ticking of a clock in the back room somewhere, hidden in the house. Elizabeth tries to drink the tea that her mother has made, but it has long since gone cold, and the chill of it constricts her throat.

"Mummy, there's something you should know." She tries to speak calmly and clearly, as she was taught at school, many years ago — many years ago, before her father went to sea and never came back, before her mother finally abandoned all hope of grandchildren. Yes, the older woman has seen all this, and she knows what Elizabeth will say.

"Say what's on your mind, child." Her mother busies herself with clearing away the supper things, rinsing dishes at the sink, emptying told tea into the drain. Elizabeth hates the dying daylight, the stain of darkness that slowly tints the sky. She feels as if she were dissolving, being swallowed by this exquisite misery of truth. Night creatures, rising from the yard's truncated grass, begin a plainsong underneath the kitchen windows.

"Mummy, when you were a girl, did you ever have a special friend?" The words are hard to say, and yet Elizabeth knows she must say them before the evening draws too dark a curtain. "One very special girlfriend, that you loved more than ever you could a sister?"

Her mother takes the teapot between her palms, her face sketched blank, without expression. "Why, yes," she says at last, "there was a girl I knew from Bonavista — her name was Louise. She married an American."

She cannot possibly understand, Elizabeth thinks. In the

gloaming, her grass-green fingernails appear bloody. "Not like that exactly, Mummy."

"I know what you mean!" Her mother sets the teapot on the sideboard with a thump. "You think I've never seen those mannish women with their hair cut off? When your father was alive, we went on holiday down to Florida. I saw two of them, walking on the street. Dressed like men, they were."

"It isn't like that!" Elizabeth cries, distressed. "Amelia and I have planned to make our lives together!"

She thinks her mother's sudden sharp intake of breath is a reaction to the confession she has made. If they permitted themselves to be demonstrative with familial affection, perhaps Elizabeth might go to her mother's side, clasp the older woman's work-weary hands in hers. Such action is of course impossible. It cannot be done. And so Elizabeth waits until her mother has gone upstairs, and then she slips into her dead brother's anorak and boots, and with the house key in her pocket, goes guiltily out into the August twilight.

The local pub is close by, only a few moments' walk, and she takes a table gratefully. She orders whisky and takes it with just a little water. She remembers Amelia's scorn for her lifelong habit of sherry and Amelia's insistence upon good whisky in their shared lodgings. A sharp and tensile loneliness assails her, and she goes out to the telephone, listening breathlessly to the disjointed ringing. "I've told my mother everything," she says. She wants Amelia to know the sacrifices she has made. She wonders if it might have been accomplished some other way. Perhaps it is wrong to tell, just as it is wrong to keep silent. She longs for the morning when the bus will take her once again into the familiar landscape of home. She cannot bear to be here any longer. She cannot bear the silences or the wordless hum of night creatures underneath the kitchen window. She cannot bear her mother's expression of silent rebuke.

"Behave yourself and study hard." Elizabeth's mother does not get out of the car; Elizabeth takes her suitcase out of the trunk herself. There is much more she wants to say and cannot: the silence is a chasm, an abyss too large to breach. She waves as Elizabeth steps aboard the bus. She waves until the bus is lost to sight, as the familiar hills and furrows of the land dissolve and blur. The yard and all its echoes are still waiting, and there is the teapot and the kitchen. The stubble fields are warm as August dies into September. There are no letters. There is nothing, after all.

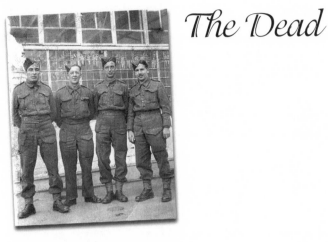

The Dead

They are all old men now, somewhere in the secret provinces of memory, all but forgotten, called up like ghosts every so often, like figures in an old photograph. There are four of them, Newfie boys, from some nameless outport that is very like Moira Doone's Guernsey, but isn't. It could be anywhere, this place they come from. It could be nowhere. It could be subject to the vagaries of memory, as they themselves are.

Arthur is to the extreme left of the photograph, gazing into the camera's lens with a kind of belligerence. What's he doing here? He's just a stupid Newfie — a wild colonial boy. He came over here to cut trees in the forestry at Aviemore and ended up in the British Army: roll call at five, standing for an hour in the freezing cold with just your skivvies on, while some pansy-arse from London with a pencil moustache ordered you around. Dickie Dunn peed himself that first cold morning: standing barefoot on the icy tarmac, hands rigid at his sides. He wasn't even shouted at, they only asked if he was having a good morning. He let fly with it, pissed all down the inside of his leg. The Captain told him to save his piss for Jerry, because he'd need it. They expected to see combat any time. Dickie isn't in this picture. I think I would recognize Dickie if I saw him. I think Dickie probably got killed early on, or else he lives, an old man, in some distant place that I have never visited. No, that can't be right. He's dead — he has to be.

Arthur and the others are standing in this picture as if waiting, casually, for something. They are pretending to be easy in their uniforms, easy in their skins, but they aren't. Behind them is some sort of building, a barracks or an aircraft hangar. They are waiting to be sent out into the war.

Arthur went to sea when he was nine, fishing with his father because it was necessary; there were a lot of little mouths to feed. His mother was always pregnant, with two or three small children at her skirts and a baby in her arms, nuzzled against her leaking breasts. The first time Arthur put to sea was on a calm June morning with the ocean like a sheet of glass and the sun rolling over the horizon, flaming red and savage. "When I tells ya, you haul," his father said, instructing him. His father hardly ever spoke; and for the balance of that first trip he and Arthur toiled in silence, hauling the nets over the side, dispatching the gasping fish into the shallow hold. And Arthur was seasick, too, bobbing in the oily swells when the wind came up, retching over the side. When his father boiled the kettle and cooked salt fish at dinnertime, Arthur ate a little, felt somewhat better. He never regretted being taken out of school because he wasn't really learning much there anyway, except how to read and how to do his sums. He hated carrying the dirty slate back and forth to school each day, hated the ignominy of the tiny sponge, the bottle of water. He despised the sight of inkwells in the desks. He couldn't be entirely sure where his future might lead, but he did not believe that it was

here, among the desks and chalk dust, listening to the mono-
tonous slosh of water against the blank face of his slate.

He thinks about the noise that water makes — now,
washing his face and hands at an anonymous barracks sink —
he remembers how it was then, the slap of ocean water against
the boat's hull, riding careless on the waves on a June morning.
What vestige of the sacrosanct was left when men like him were
taken from the ocean, sent thousands of miles away to die? He
wonders, or feels that he ought to wonder, what the war will
finally be like when he gets to see it up close, recognizable. He
thinks about the sea a lot, and at night in his dreams he is back
there again, his feet forced against the uneven rolling backbone
of the boat, and beneath it, the cold salt sea. He is alone out
there, as he imagines he will be when he is sent Over the Top.
What an odd expression it is, a kind of chant that one feels
certain of remembering, a chant that one might want to repeat
over and over again. He finds himself repeating it: "Over the
Top, boys!" late at night as he lies on his thin-framed barracks
bunk, waiting as he always does for sleep to take him. He
thinks that he should fall asleep to the imagined roar of
cannons, but he doesn't. He falls asleep instead to the gentle
slap and susurration of the waves against the keel.

He remembers the snow and how it used to fall on that
outport that isn't Guernsey, but might be. He always liked the
winter, liked the way a sudden squall could blur things round
the edges. But there was fear in it as well: the fear of being
caught at sea when a sudden gale of wind blew up, driving the
snow before it, blinding them. There was a chance that you
might run up on the rocks before you had time to get your
bearings, be dashed to pieces. It was the reverse of darkness,
the wrong side of a photographic plate: things white themselves

appeared strange to it. A gull might be a phantasm, a ghostly embrace.

He thinks of these things as he falls asleep.

Hurley occupies the barracks bunk directly below Arthur. Hurley is as tall and thin as a decapitated sunflower, with gangly pipe stick arms and legs. He comes from down around Fortune Bay and speaks with the same Cornish cadence that Arthur grew up listening to. Hurley is afraid to die — he isn't ashamed to say it — because he comes from a big family, and if he dies his father cannot make ends meet. Hurley has several brothers, all younger, all afraid that Hurley will die before he has made their living for them. He tells Arthur these things as they lie in their beds at night, listening to the drone of aircraft engines as another squadron bellies up to the tarmac, disappears into a blacked-out sky. Hurley wants to get out of the war alive so he can go back home, wait until his father dies and inherit the keeping of the rest. He tells Arthur that he wants to add a piece on to his father's house, find himself a nice girl and settle down.

Arthur wonders what he wants to do when the war is over. He doesn't tell Hurley about the Scottish girl he's met, and how they've been dating on the q.t. whenever Arthur can get a weekend pass. Her name is Dorothy, and she is at this very moment in the midst of a cataclysmic divorce. She has a daughter two years old, and she will leave her behind in Scotland when she and Arthur marry and hurry back to Newfoundland. The little girl is curiously silent. When Arthur tries to speak to her, she turns her face away. She knows that this man will take her Mam away. She knows that she will be left behind. In later life, after Dorothy's own mother dies, and the child is left alone, she will harbour an acute resentment against Arthur and against Dorothy, too. But all that is still in the future. The little girl will never know her parents — and later, when there is a sister and a brother, she will hate them bitterly, without ever having seen them. It's just the way things are. She knows all of this already: it's all locked up, deep inside her childish heart.

They see combat first of all in Africa: hotter than Arthur's most vividly imagined Hell, a desert, empty and scalded, scoured clean. The Captain tells them to check their boots every morning for scorpions that can kill with their sting. They are given two pints of water a day. They can shave with it, wash with it, or drink it. No one washes, and all the men grow beards. In addition, they are provided with salt tablets to prevent dehydration. Arthur feels as though he is being bleached by the sun, as though all the moisture in his body were being squeezed out, forced from his pores. He turns red at first, then brown, and his beard grows wild and unruly. At night, when the desert is a flat bowl of moonlight, he runs reconnaissance, looking for Rommel and never finding him. He awakens in the morning, weary from strange dreams, and thinks of Dorothy. He wonders what she would think if she could see him now. His blue eyes stare, maddened, out of his crisp brown face, and when he dutifully eats his salt, he believes that he can taste the ocean. He wonders how long the war will last. He wonders if he will get out alive.

There are letters, but the mail is slow in coming and must be vetted by the censors. Arthur receives letters from home with large pieces cut out: a paragraph in his mother's crabbed and childish handwriting, talking about the turnips and the seaweed and the potato ground. When he looks around, all he can see are monstrous waves of sand that shift and change position almost imperceptibly. Their movement might merely be imagined, and sometimes, when Arthur glances out of the corners of his eyes, he fancies that there *is* something moving just beyond the arc of his perception. The sands play tricks on him; they sift into his nostrils and his hair, fill the insides of his boots while he is sleeping. They cast a net of sparkling particles over him as he sleeps; he cannot escape them.

There is a letter from Dorothy, handwritten on blue paper, taut and crackling. It is dated three months ago, and he realizes that in the rest of the world it's still winter. He wonders what his family did at Christmas. Unlike the other letters, this one has somehow slipped through the trap set by the censors. It comes to him whole: a single page in Dorothy's handwriting, telling him absolutely nothing. The little girl, whose name (he learns) is Maggie, has had a birthday party with cake and presents. Arthur is glad he missed it. The child makes him nervous. Of herself Dorothy says nothing, but wishes him well and inquires, oddly enough, after news of his family. She doesn't ask about Arthur himself, and it's just as well. Loose talk is taboo, and anyway, he cannot ever find the words to tell Dorothy or anyone about the desert.

He begins to be obsessed with the sand, can't get it out of his mind. He tries not to think of it, tries to ignore it, but is unable to. He is forced to regard the sand in a certain manner, following certain rituals. These are similar to things he made himself do at home when he was a boy. He enacts them now, as he did back then, as he did every morning before setting foot in his father's boat. He does it for the same reason: to preserve his life, to save himself. He must turn to all four directions immediately upon rising each morning and contemplate the horizon. He must strain his eyes, peering into the hard, shimmering distance, making sure. He begins to feel that he is part of the desert, that he and the sand are made of the same things, the same sparkling particles.

Before long their ranks are thinned by various assaults and skirmishes. The Captain strolls among them before each battle, reassuring them, while Arthur watches the horizon rigidly. And then the Captain is killed in a pre-dawn raid, and they are left alone, it seems, rudderless in the desert. A letter comes from Dorothy, heavily censored, the whole of it held together with tape, and what little writing there is becomes obscured. Arthur feels as though he must piece meaning out of it. Dorothy is telling him about a dress she has bought, a dress she hopes to wear when he comes home again. He thinks about her standing on a chair in her kitchen, drawing a fake seam down the back of each leg with an eyebrow pencil. There are no stockings to be had. Arthur examines the date at the top of the letter using it to orient himself, but he can't. The dunes are always there, and time has no meaning in this place. He loses her letter — perhaps on purpose — perhaps he lets it fall onto the sparkling net of sand. Perhaps the wind blows it away. He is losing himself here. He is losing all of himself; he is disappearing into the sands of the desert, blowing away on the wind.

When the war is over, when he is extracted from the desert as if by strange summoning, he mourns for it. He feels that it has sifted itself into his blood or settled like ashes in the marrow of his bones. He goes back to Scotland when they are demobbed, goes back to Dorothy, who greets him with the diffidence expected of the newly widowed. Her inconvenient husband has conveniently got himself killed at Tripoli. Dorothy's divorce, begun before she and Arthur met, is no longer necessary. She will marry him and go to Newfoundland, where she will bear him two children and devote her life to dictating the terms of his existence.

Maggie will be left behind in Scotland — like Arthur's memories of the desert, the ocean, and the war.

The Holy Stones

Here is Edna and here is Alec, here are the holy Stones — the East End Stones, in the East End of old St. John's or somewhere like it, the grandmother and grandfather of someone no one knows. The buildings in the background look like army barracks, and so perhaps this was taken in the good old days, when Newfoundland was still such a bastion of Empire. Such a very British back yard, Brittania at its best, laid out in rows of poky little houses, narrow alleys lined with filth and pigeons, and doorsteps grimed with soot and coal dust. Edna is glad to have it and so is Alec, for he comes from the Southern Shore and knows a thing or two about deprivation. Here is a socket he can fit to — here is a receptacle for people like Alec and Edna Stone. They are grateful to God for all His myriad blessings, even when the kitchen wall fell down and when Edna lost a breast to cancer. They are forever mindful of how much worse it could be, of how bad things are apt to get. They are figures in a picture, as sharp and clear as stereopticon. They are no one that anyone knows. They are no one's relations, no one's ancestors.

Edna was the first one to forsake the religion of her child-hood and venture out to the weekly meetings at the Evangel Temple on Suvla Street. She only went there because Doris Bastow, two stony backyards over, shouted about it at the communal clothesline two Mondays before last. "They let all sorts in," she'd said to Edna, "whoever wants to come, there's a place for them."

Doris likes it because there's plenty of music, and they shake tambourines like the harem girls do in the movies at the cinema. It's a bit of a change from the C of E, Doris says (or rather, shouts) and why doesn't Edna just come along and find out for herself?

Edna does. She unearths an old straw hat, transfixed with many pins, and forces her arthritic feet into her good black shoes. "You're going to that queer old church with Doris Bastow, aren't ye?" Alec doesn't even look up from his news-paper. He's reading: the Commission of Government and all its doings, the Hope Simpsons at the Hotel Newfoundland complaining about their cramped accommodations. Alec sees himself in this and other stereotypes, imagines himself to be descended from a long line of Englishmen reaching back to the Battle of the Boyne. "That Doris Bastow is soft in the head."

Edna has learned to ignore him, and anyway, she wants to hear the energetic music and see the tambourines being shaken by the harem girls. She wants to sample some part of life that is foreign to her. She wants to see what Doris Bastow finds to shout about, leaning over clotheslines.

The meetings are held in an old, ramshackle union hall, with a motley assortment of chairs placed in rows and a makeshift podium situated at the front of the building. Edna arrives with Doris Bastow, who is dressed in a plain black frock that smells vaguely of mothballs. Edna has tried to find out what the service will be like, but Doris simply tells her that it's "a bit different." This could mean anything, Edna thinks — there could be dancing or wild moaning, or there might be snakes brought out of boxes for the worshippers to fondle. She isn't sure that she should stay for this, and besides, what would Alec think if she were bitten by a snake and couldn't make his breakfast in the morning?

The minister is a shabby little man in an ill-fitting shiny suit with patches of some darker fabric at the elbows and mending at the knees. He is suspiciously oily-looking, as though he has been greased all over by some mysterious process. His hands move about incessantly, making fluttering movements near his face as the singing begins. The music consists of a blond man with a guitar and a face full of pimples, and a studious-looking girl with long, straight hair, who hits a tambourine against her thighs, listlessly. Edna waits for harem girls, but there aren't any, and when the congregation rises to sing, she is disappointed that the selection is merely "Lead, Kindly Light" and not some weird collection of barks and grunts.

The interesting bit comes during the sermon, when the oily little minister descends from the platform and ranges through the crowd, searching deep into the eyes of the congregation. Near the front, two women about Edna's age fall down in a dead faint as he passes by, and a teenaged boy leaps up onto his chair and raises his arms high above his head, as though seeking some impetus for flight. He will crash into the congregation, Edna thinks and tries to turn away, but she cannot tear her eyes from the spectacle. She feels as though something miraculous is about to happen, and she cannot bear to miss it. The young girl on the platform goes on slamming the tambourine against her thighs, a rhythmic noise, and the boy with the guitar and the pimples begins to strum harder and harder. The music is pulsing inside her head, and Edna cannot bear it. Her feet begin to tap, out of sight beneath her chair, and her whole body is shaking. She clamps her lips closed, determined not to give in to it, determined not to sing or shout, but her hands are clapping in time to the addictive chant. Doris Bastow has tears streaming down her face as the oily minister comes by, his fluttering hands making careful patterns in the air. He leans close to Doris Bastow, his nose scant inches from her heaving bosom. "Will you be saved?" he asks. "Will you be washed in the Blood of the Lamb?"

Edna watches as Doris leaps to her feet, her body a mass of jiggling flesh underneath her dowdy frock. She raises her hands in the air and does a kind of dance, shrieking at intervals, accompanied by tambourine and guitar. Edna watches in silence, her feet still hidden underneath her chair, still tapping madly in an invisible rhythm all her own.

Alec is still reading the paper at the kitchen table when she arrives back home. The oily minister and his halo-faced acolytes have disappeared into the outer darkness of an East End night. The sound of the clock resonates throughout the front hallway as Edna lets herself in. She sets the kettle on the stove and takes the pins out of her hat carefully, folding her gloves inside the pockets of her coat. "Doris Bastow got saved," she says to Alec. "At the meeting tonight." She does not tell Alex what Doris confided to her on the way home: that Doris gets saved every night, because she loves the hypnotic beat of the tambourines, the way the guitar leaps and throbs, the ragged, atonal singing of the congregation.

Alec grunts, absorbed in the fortunes of various local

businessmen, the rise and fall of coal prices, the cost of car fare. He has already read part of the paper, and Edna takes this up with her as she ascends the stairs in darkness. The Commission of Government and Sir John and Lady Hope Simpson accompany her to bed, wait patiently as she folds herself into her nightdress, sipping gratefully from her cup. She thinks about the tambourine and the guitar. She thinks that she will go down again next Tuesday night, and she wonders what Alex will say. She wonders if Alec will say anything at all.

Effie's Landwash

Whenever she thinks about the future, she imagines herself in a white saltbox house high upon the cliffs above the landwash, all alone. She is never really sure *why* she imagines herself as being that way, but every time the image comes to her it's the same: the white saltbox house, its windows and their curtains, and the strong scent of sage growing near the front door. In this private kind of dream, it's always a windy summer day, and she's pinning laundry on the line. The laundry, like the house, is white. The grass is a verdurous, sharp green. Behind the house, beyond the convex swell of the land, she can see the sun-bright wave tops sparkling as they are dashed against the cliffs, hurtling themselves to death. Beyond the hill itself and beyond the portion of the waves that she can see, the ocean is roaring like a November gale. This is how she would like her life to be: austere, protected, surrounded by the ocean and the hills.

Of course, it isn't like that — life rarely follows any sort of wishing — there are no schemes. It's like looking at pictures of bathing suits in the Eaton's catalogue and imagining that a

Newfoundland summer will look like that — that there will be the sun, and blazing heat, and sandy beaches. Mostly, she worries about money, because her husband Ches works for the Highways, and there's talk that there might be layoffs coming. She doesn't know what she will have to do if something like this happens, but she can imagine it very well. She will have to move away from here, leave her child in the care of Chester's mother, and go to St. John's to find work in a factory making sweet biscuits, rubber tires or bread. This wouldn't be quite so bad, except — there is her painting.

This is a secret no one knows, not even Ches. She has always been an artist, even in this place, where such pursuits are frowned upon, thought to be airy-fairy, not real. *What's real?* she wonders. She knows that only tangible things merit attention: the ability to bake a perfect partridgeberry pie, a talent for fine crochet or needlework. Painting — especially the kind of painting that Effie does — is regarded with suspicion. Effie paints the landscape in all its terrifying beauty. She doesn't want to lose this intense and personal view, this sense of paramount connection. When the child is asleep in the afternoons, Effie takes the pram and goes to the hills that overlook the landwash. She spreads her brushes out, carefully chooses one, steadies the flat canvas on her knees. She needs to capture the landscape as it is, before the water and the wind have changed it. She works quickly, sketching the contours of the hills, the muscular sea. While she works, she is immersed in it, immersed in the summer landscape. Often, there is a white saltbox house placed somewhere on the canvas. While the child sleeps beside her, dreaming infant dreams, Effie inhabits the mystical landscape, the landwash of her dreams, and she is happier than she is anywhere else — happier than in her waking life. She never wants to live in any other space than this. Some part of her knows and instinctively rejects the world of matter and form, the world that would separate her from this thing that she loves above everything — more than her bones and skin and hair, more than the air that lines the pockets of her flesh.

But real events intrude, as they so often do, and one night Effie is setting the table for supper when Ches comes home and relays the inevitable: several of the men have been let go, and although his own job is still intact, there are more layoffs to come and nothing to say that he will not be next. He offers her this news in the same way he always does, as if expecting her to do something about it, leap up immediately and announce that she will sell as much Avon as it takes, or bake pies for the autumn fair, as many pies as anyone can stand. He expects her to say that she has just that moment been elected president of Ford, and she will make a million dollars. *Why don't you get a job*, he says, and Effie always thinks, *I've got a job. I'm an artist.*

She would never dare to say this out loud. She has experienced his temper, knows it far too well to try that sort of self-affirming stand. Many times throughout their scant married life, he has shouted his frustrations at her, demanded to know why she couldn't take a job in the fish plant like all the other women did, or go down to the beach to spread fish upon the flakes for some St. John's merchant. Other women did it, he told her, other women helped their husbands. He didn't understand that some kinds of help were not hers to offer, she couldn't sell herself that way, not unless things got truly desperate. If it came to that, if they were hungry and there was no way to make the groceries, feed the child — then she would. She was not so proud or selfish as to let catastrophe strike at them.

She escapes as often as she can to the cliffs above the landwash, carrying the canvas under her arm while one hand hoists the child, now grown enough to no longer need naps in the afternoon. She spreads a blanket on the grass and lets the child sit beside her while her hand moves rapidly across the blankness, sketching in the outlines of the landscape. She draws the hills, the abrupt drop of rock and tactile air, the sudden plunge into oblivion. The child plays as she does this, and Effie sketches with only part of her mind. The majority of her thoughts are taken up with the burden of her worries: Ches will be laid off, and Effie knows she is pregnant again. Pregnant — after she had secretly vowed that this one child would be her only offspring. She has known for several months now, even though she has not yet begun to show. She will have to tell Ches very soon.

She wonders, as she sketches in the details of the landscape, whether she might do something about it. On her own she would have no idea, but surely there must be books that one could get, or some old women who could utter charms over it, banish it like putting away a wart. Just last night, as they were getting into bed, Ches said that Florence Tulk up to the dry goods store was looking for some help, and why didn't Effie go on up and put a word in for herself? Every time he suggests such things, Effie feels the bottom of her stomach contract into a fist-shape. A nameless fear claws its way up into her throat, paralyzing her. She can never speak to him, and if she did he wouldn't listen. She can never say, *I've already got a job. I'm an artist.* She could never get those words out of her mouth, could never push them past her lips, her clenched and desperate teeth. She wonders if this reluctance to expose herself to the mundane world is obstinacy or selfishness. She doesn't want to be selfish. She loves her husband. At night, when she is still awake, she leans over him and listens to the cadence of his breathing, measuring his respirations to her own. He does not know that he is cherished. He would laugh at Effie if she tried to tell him. She feels this debt of love sometimes, lying there in bed between them, a formless presence. She feels it pressing down on her, this love she has, this otherness, this formality of souls. She feels that it might smother her. She feels that she is smothering already.

When Ches comes in for dinner, he is happy and smiling, and Effie feels a sense of calm. Perhaps he has found another job, something with better pay, that will negate the necessity of certain ruin and make them safe, as safe as houses. She is more attentive than usual, bringing extra bread, extra potatoes, stirring his tea for him. She can tell him about the baby now. She can show him all her pictures of the landwash. She can show him how she paints the same white saltbox house, over and over, as if dreaming it to life. She can confess the truth about the house, that it has appeared to her, a vision.

"I spoke to Flo, up to the dry goods store this morning." He is adding extra sugar to his tea. His face is bent. He cannot see her expression. "She's going to take on a woman to help out in the shop. I knowed you was interested."

Effie cannot feel her feet and hands. She thinks that she is holding a dish, but she can't be sure. It might be air or water that she's holding, or a stone.

"She said you can start the morrow morning. Mother said she'll look out to the youngster for ye." He is pleased with himself. She can discern something in his eyes, a surfeit of glee. He is not a bad man. She knows this and repeats it to herself, so that there will be no taint of guilt left after her, no trailing ribbon of shame like blood. He is her husband, and he loves her. He cannot know that he is doing her to death by inches. He doesn't even ask her what she thinks but goes on stirring up his tea and drinking it with every evidence of great enjoyment. Effie takes his plate away and scrapes it into the garbage, lays her own uneaten supper in the pantry. While he is playing with the child in the sitting room, she gathers up her brushes and a clean white canvas and goes out by the back door, climbing swiftly up the rise, until the house behind her is nearly lost to sight. There is a grassy hillock that she would sit upon, but this isn't what she wants now. She wanders up and down the ragged stretch of the landwash, until she finds a crumbling cliff and an awful gorge open to the waves and the wind.

She begins as she has always done, laying strokes of blackness deep into the canvas. The wind is rising, dinning uproar into her bones, and she knows she must hurry, knows that she must finish quickly. She cannot see the ragged outlines of the coastline in the dark, and sight, especially, is necessary. She must fill her vision with the elemental taste of sea and stone. She must finish what she started.

She thinks she sees the house, the clapboard white and gleaming, the laundry flapping in the breeze, the rising wind. Her feet are bare, although she cannot remember kicking off her shoes, and the rain is pelting down, filling up her opened eyes. As soon as it is safe to leap, she does: falling faster than a stone, plummeting into the wash and flex of the sighing, reaching waves. She feels her body merging with the landscape, dissolving into nothing, rising up into the rain, evaporating. She is coming apart. She is weighted down with stones. She is a pocket full of sorrow.

The San

Delores, Florrie and June were never friends in the traditional sense of the word, despite what the picture looks like. Here they are, standing with arms linked, in front of a woodframe building, vaguely institutional. Delores is at the left of the photo, her dark hair in an improbable pouf, her dress a shapeless, gunnysack affair. Her feet disappear somewhere into the snowy floorboards of the porch, and you get the sense that she is slowly melting — melting as the rotten, late-winter snow is melting.

Apart from Florrie, the youngest (she is in the centre of the photo) none of the women are wearing coats or mittens, and so I surmise that this must have been taken when winter was ending, for who would allow three TB patients to stand outdoors in a freezing cold? Who would be the arbiter of such cruelty, so carelessly dispensed? They are standing in front of the Sanatorium — the San — and they don't seem to be ill or dying, but they are.

There is an old lady at the San, called Mrs. Ragnell. Delores, Florrie and June regard her with something very like horror, something akin to loathing, for she's indeed quite loathly. She is ancient, a hunchbacked crone with sunken cheeks and skin as seamed and creased as old leather. Not only is Dame Ragnell dying of the lingering consumption, but she is also a cripple: years of unchecked diabetes have whittled away the flesh of her lower limbs, and where she once had feet there are now merely blackened and necrotic stumps. She is what they might eventually become. She is the truth they cannot bear to face.

Delores, Florrie and June do everything together, are always engaged in great campaigns of whispering, huddled together in the sunporch, their hands cupped around their mouths, blowing on their fingers. It will be another three months before any hint of heat steals into the San, and even then it will be carefully screened out by drapes, hidden from view. Too much excitement will only make the dying more distraught, and anyway — if they wish to bask in light then they can do it in the chapel where the multicoloured panes diffuse it into harmless blobs of colour.

Mrs. Ragnell scares the living daylights out of Delores, Florrie and June, and this is why they feel justified in tormenting her. They plan these escapades with as much thought as if they were preparing to scale Everest; they lie in wait for Mrs. Ragnell, plant surprises for her, rejoice in the results. They show no modesty, for in this place with its unrelieved whiteness, with its smell of illness and disinfectant, there is no need. Florrie leaves her soiled Kotex in the drawer beside Mrs. Ragnell's bed, the menstrual evidence festering in the artificial heat. The trio thinks this is very funny, and they scream with laughter to hear Florrie tell it over and over again. Mrs. Ragnell, furious to the point of apoplexy, wheels after Florrie, down the hallway, shouting curses and screaming like a harridan. Her truncated feet stick out at the end of the wheelchair's footrests, bandage-wrapped and wholly horrible. By her very ugliness, she brings punishment upon herself.

But this is relatively minor when laid against the theft of Mrs. Ragnell's rosary beads, which Delores steals and wears about her waist like a belt, the heavy cross swinging like the tolling of a bell. They mark the floor beside Mrs. Ragnell's bed with lipstick, hide her false teeth in the toilet, and dangle her brassiere out the window of the Doctors' restroom. They think it's all enormous fun, and after all, Mrs. Ragnell could make herself a bit more amenable, could put forward an effort to be friendly, but she doesn't. She hides behind corners, in bathrooms. She arms herself with a heavy walking stick and flails at the girls as they pass by. She raises bruises on their legs and screams with laughter when they trip.

One day, towards spring, when the snow is melting and running away, Florrie is told that she isn't getting any better. Here in the San, such pronouncements aren't surprising, for everyone who comes here expects, somewhere at the back of her mind, that she will either die or carry on in a lingering state, a sort of gradual fading, a blurring of the edges. Delores and Jane aren't there when Florrie receives her diagnosis, and she is left to bear it all alone. She believes it is a strange accident of fate and, being rather more introspective than the other two, wonders what she might have done. Perhaps she ought to have been more respectful towards Mrs. Ragnell? Florrie thinks about this, sitting on her narrow hospital bed, her thin legs, pale to translucence, set out in front of her as though they were nothing more than a couple of sticks. Lesions on the lungs, her doctor said. Tubercular matter present throughout the digestive tract. It's true that Florrie hasn't felt like eating much lately. She has grown to rather like her newly gaunt look, and thinks about starlets in the 1920s, who had ribs and bones removed, striving for the illusion of eternal youth and beauty.

She avoids Delores and June, begins to spend her time at the far end of the ward, sitting by a sunlit window, twirling her hair around her fingers. She wonders what is happening to her body: how invisible cells or particles of matter are growing wantonly inside it. She casts about her for something she might do about it, but there isn't anything, of course. There isn't anything at all. It is inevitable, like the rotten, late-winter snow that melts and falls away. Delores and June make several attempts to draw her out — token gestures, really, for she is marked for death now, and this is something they want no part of. They came to the San because they had to. They want to leave here walking, not carried out like late victims of some modern plague. This isn't them — they want no part of it. They leave Florrie to her own devices, leave her to her contemplation and her late-made pieties.

Now there is only Florrie — and Mrs. Ragnell, the loathly lady, wheeling hell-bent for leather around the corridors, wielding her stick like a policeman's truncheon. Mrs. Ragnell is dying too. Perhaps she and Florrie might be carried out together, women alone, women crouching under sheets and waiting for a resurrection. Florrie knows that she will die, and even has some idea of the manner of her death. She knows it will not be painful, but merely a loss of breath close to the end, a gradual sinking into darkness. She wonders most of all about what comes after — after the last breath has heaved the body closed, after the eyelids have been shut, after the body pours away its facile fluids, its bones and muscle-meat. She wonders what it might feel like, when, taking that last breath, she dives under the surface, never to rise again.

"You looks some sick." This from Mrs. Ragnell, who is

hardly a model of dewy health herself. Today she has risen from her wheelchair as though defying illness, and is rather unsteadily mounted on two wooden crutches. "We all goes that way in the end. I guess I'll be going soon enough." She seats herself by Florrie, watching the spring rain fall outside the open window. The air is pungent with the smell of the greening hills. She understands why Florrie has left the window open. "What'd the doctor say, my darlin'?" Mrs. Ragnell is trying to be friendly and maternal, Florrie thinks, and she remembers the menstrual pads, secreted in Mrs. Ragnell's drawer, and all the other nasty pranks she played in company with June and Delores. She wonders why Mrs. Ragnell should be nice to her. She wonders if she can survive such niceness. It's more than anyone has ever given her in here — more than she expected.

"I'm not going to get better." Florrie feels as if she's said this about a hundred times, chanted it like an oratory response, clutched it to her like a talisman. The words seem to have a strange flavour on her palate, a sprinkling of ashes — the taste of something drained of substance. She imagines that the ashes have been deposited there by some occult means, and she wonders which one of them has done it. She wants to ask Mrs. Ragnell about the secret things, about the last moments of the body, but the words stick in her throat.

She listens to the sound of the spring rain, splashing on the windowsill, and thinks that death must be a little bit like breathing.

Definitely Somewhere

Dennis and his sister Sheila love swimming, and most of all they love going to the Pond. The ocean is too cold to swim in, and it numbs the bones, chills the flesh to insensibility. The Pond is warm, with a bottom of small pebbles and fine sand, the processed bones of ancient boulders. The Pond has no other name; it has always been known simply as the Pond, and if it ever had a name, no one remembers. It's where everyone goes to swim and sunbathe in the brief Newfoundland summer. It's where Dennis and Sheila are today, with their Aunt Deal, whose name is actually Delia, but who, like the Pond, has accepted this dubious nomenclature. Dennis and Sheila's parents are "on the Mainland for work" which is actually a euphemism for "run away and left their children." This is why Aunt Deal takes them to the Pond, because they live with her, and because there is no one else.

Their parents, also named Dennis and Sheila, left when the children were both quite young. At last report they were in Guelph, Ontario, or perhaps Nova Scotia, picking apples in a vast and secret orchard. They were definitely somewhere on the Mainland, that much was absolutely known. Sheila waits hopefully for a letter from them, but there is never anything in the mail except bills and catalogues. She enjoys looking through this latter item, especially at the photographs of ladies in their swimsuits, lounging on an artificial beach underneath a Mainland sun. She has already decided which swimsuit she will choose to take to the Mainland when her mother comes to fetch her back, and she has already decided how chic and elegant she will appear, lounging on an artificial beach under a Toronto sun. Sheila is sure that her mother will call her on the weekend. It doesn't matter which weekend. Dennis tells everyone his father is gone up north, hunting polar bears, and that he will come home with lots of furs, perhaps worth a million dollars, or close enough. He says this to all the boys at school who like to tease him. When his arguments are unsuccessful there are schoolyard scuffles and fistfights, anger surging to the surface when he confronts them all on the library steps or in the lunchroom. Peggy Norris tells him that his father is a gambler and a drunk and his mother is a whore, and that's why they ran away, before the Mounties could come and catch them. Peggy Norris is a girl, and this is why Dennis isn't allowed to hit her, so when he finds Artie Critch in the lunchroom by himself, he smacks him in the head, relishing the brittle crunch of his bony knuckles against little Artie's skull. If Dennis were older and had the language for it, he might wonder why he gets so angry all the time. But Dennis is thirteen, and he can't accurately vocalize the wash of heat and shame that crawls up from his gullet whenever people ask about his parents. He cannot say for certain where they are — he only know that they are definitely somewhere, somewhere other than here.

Dennis never tells Aunt Deal these things, because she's

always sighing and complaining. Aunt Deal isn't married, and Dennis wonders if it's because she sighs so much. Maybe husbands only want a laughing girl, or a quiet girl who'd let them speak. Aunt Deal, when she isn't sighing, is a telephone operator at the local exchange. She talks all day. At night, when Dennis and Sheila have done their homework, Aunt Deal is still talking, often to herself. Her voice moves up and down the stairwell, and down into the basement where the jars of jam are kept, and the precious loaves of homemade bread. She talks even if no one is listening, even if no one cares. And she never laughs or smiles. Whenever Dennis or his sister venture a complaint, Aunt Deal sighs more heavily than before and launches into a lengthy discourse on how she is doing her Duty by them, and how their parents, God bless 'em, couldn't do their Duty, so she, Aunt Deal, has to do her Duty. Sheila isn't sure what this weighty word entails, or what it might require of a person, but it sounds mighty unpleasant, like medicine taken at bedtime to stave off tapeworms. Dennis had a tapeworm last summer, and Aunt Deal told him it was because Perry Tucker dared him to eat sheep shit out behind the Loyal Orange Lodge, and Dennis did it. Sheila asked Dennis if eating sheep shit out behind the Lodge constituted some sort of Duty, but Dennis told her to shut up and go to sleep. Dennis had to endure several long visits to Dr. So, the Chinese doctor up the shore, who peered down his throat with a long instrument and nearly made him vomit. This gave Dennis much to brag about to his friends and contemporaries, about how the chink had drove a pitchfork down his gullet and hauled his guts out.

Mostly, life with Aunt Deal is fairly benign. Aunt Deal does not drink in secret, or smoke cigarettes, or play cards, or entertain gentlemen callers of any persuasion. Several years before, Morris Hickey had made a temporary practice of showing up on Aunt Deal's doorstep of a summer evening, clutching a handful of piss-a-beds, smelling of cheap cologne, and hoping for what Dennis called a rawn-de-voose. Aunt Deal would meet him at the door, barefoot and in her shabby housedress, her hair bristling with a quantity of brush rollers, and ask him what in the Name of the World he wanted. Dennis said that Aunt Deal and Morris Hickey were going up behind the Loyal Orange Lodge to have a rawn-de-voose, but Sheila didn't think Aunt Deal would like that sort of thing. She had visions of Aunt Deal, in her cotton housedress, with her bristly rollers, draped over skinny Morris Hickey, thrashing in the fresh sheep shit, green and teeming with tapeworms. No, Aunt Deal wouldn't like that sort of thing at all. Whenever Morris showed up with his sweaty bouquet of piss-a-beds, Aunt Deal sent him on his way. "I haven't got time to be frigging around with the likes of you," she'd say. "And your poor wife not even cold in the ground." Morris's wife Nellie had died about ten years before, when she drove Morris's pickup truck off the end of the Government Wharf one night in November. Everybody said that Nellie had a brain tumour, but Aunt Deal had been heard to say that Morris drove her to it — that he ought to wear the aftershave once in awhile instead of drinking it, and maybe poor old Nellie wouldn't have gone right off her head. All this was the drama of their lives, played out against the backdrop of the outport, where nothing much happened, and whenever something did happen, everybody knew about it. Sheila and Dennis, if asked, would never have admitted to being happy, but in truth, they were. Aunt Deal acted as some sort of buffer between them and the outside world; she blocked all heinous influences with her sighing and her talking and her stolid, blocky body. Aunt

Deal could and would protect them from any dominion under God or Man. She was reliable in the way few people are, or can be, when pressed for choice.

Aunt Deal is waiting for them when they come home from school, which is very strange, because Aunt Deal is usually at work until suppertime, and Dennis and Sheila must occupy themselves accordingly, with homework or household chores. Aunt Deal is not dressed as she normally is for work, which is also very strange. She is sitting in a kitchen chair beside the window, looking out onto the straight dirt road that trails along in front of the house, leading to the shop, the post office. Her hands are folded in her lap, and her feet, shod in new black shoes, are crossed at the ankles. She is dressed for church or for a funeral, and there is even a dab of bright red lipstick on her mouth. She does not meet them at the door; she does not even move or stand, and until Sheila bends to look into her shuttered face, she is insensible.

"We got to go into town," Aunt Deal says. The lipsticked mouth is like a gash in her pale face, a bloody hole.

"I'm going out to play hockey with Trevor —"

Dennis barely has this out of his mouth before Aunt Deal crushes it. "We got to go into town," she says, "and Frank is coming with the taxi."

"Trevor wants —"

"Go wash your face and hands, both of ye. And put on decent clothes. Sheila, wash your feet, for the love of God." Aunt Deal is suddenly in motion, and things assume a patina of normalcy as she ushers them down the hall to the bathroom, fills the sink, presses washcloths and soap upon them. She is everywhere at once: in the bedrooms, muttering through the chest of drawers, and in the closet, finding shoes and socks and dresses. Sheila submits to a rough-and-ready toilette, endures Aunt Deal's savage face washing and obediently slides her feet into shoes. She is made to wear her Sunday best, though Aunt Deal is United and they never go to church, even when the minister comes from Hartleyville. She hopes Aunt Deal will not force her to wear the silly Easter hat with the elastic band that bites into her neck, and fortunately this is not the case. They are piled into the dusty black hearse that passes for a taxi, and even before the car has left the town Dennis is making faces, ramming his fingers up his nose and pulling out snots that he forces Sheila to examine. Aunt Deal sits in the front seat beside the spindly, lanky form of Frank, who used to be the undertaker before Phil Green opened up his funeral home. Next to Frank, Aunt Deal seems huge, as colossal as a mountain, and formidable. She sits bolt upright, even through the swaying of the car, and does not move until St. John's looms up in the distance.

She turns to look at them, her eyes curiously pale and flat, her lipsticked mouth a bloody smear. She has touched her mouth at least once with her gloved hand, for the fingers are red and stained with the colour, and the flesh underneath her chin has shed its powder onto the black collar of her suit coat.

"Where's we going, Aunt Deal?" Sheila has watched the landscape sliding by, out the window of the car. She has only ever been to town once in her life, and she wonders why they're going now.

"We're going to see your mother and father."

Sheila thinks about polar bears and the stories that Dennis likes to tell; she can't remember what her mother looks like, or how tall her father might be. "What for?"

"Dennis, get your fingers out of your nose." Aunt Deal rams a tissue against his face, holds it there until he blows as if his eyes will pop out. "We're going to see your parents. They're back home. They wants to see you."

Sheila wonders what this means. As much as she wants to believe in it as something good, something wished and hoped for, the idea of it torments and savages her. She watches out the window, pretending interest in the passing city. She will not cry. She will never cry, she tells herself. Only babies cry, and she is not a baby but a big girl, nearly eleven. She ignores the sound of Dennis snuffling on the other side of the car. Dennis isn't crying, either. Sheila wonders when Aunt Deal found out and who told her. She imagines there must have been a phone call or a letter of some kind, a telegram. Perhaps Aunt Deal sensed it, like some animals can sense an impending earthquake. Perhaps Aunt Deal has invisible antennae that extend into the upper atmosphere, picking up the waves of thoughts and images that emanate from the surface of the earth.

The taxi finally lands them at a red brick building, stark and imposing, with tall windows made of gleaming glass, fixed in place by iron bars. Dennis blinks in the deepening twilight, like some creature recently unearthed from the depths, and stumbles on the set of concrete steps that lead up to the entrance. Sheila sneaks a glance at him: his face is bloated and puffy, his cheeks and eyelids swollen. She knows he has been crying, but loyalty ensures her silence. She follows Aunt Deal's broad back along the narrow corridors until they find themselves standing in a stark white bedroom, with a dark-haired woman on a bed, dressed in a faded cotton housedress, her feet encased in woolly socks.

Sheila has no memories to conjure her into reality, and she cannot understand what Aunt Deal might mean by bringing her to see this woman. She is conscious of her Sunday dress, its unfamiliar cotton stiffness, the brush of hair underneath her chin and down her back. She curtsies as she has been taught at school, wishes the woman a good afternoon. She knows that as long as she is on her best behaviour, everything will be just fine. This is something to be endured, something to be braved and weathered, like the waves of the ocean. *Good afternoon,* she says, whispering it inside her mind. She cannot bear to see the woman for any longer than a moment because there is something in the vacant eyes that reminds her of Aunt Deal, something that no longer has Aunt Deal's crisp efficiency but retains a familiarity nonetheless. *Good afternoon,* she thinks, *I hope you are enjoying the lovely weather, good afternoon.* She notes the sound of her brother's footsteps, moving quickly from the room, hurrying his body away. She imagines him running down the flights of stairs, pelting out into the September darkness, seeking solace. She curtsies, and moves to take the woman's hand, smiles into the vacant eyes. *Good afternoon, and how are you?*

In coming years she will recall this moment but without significance. She will file it away, somewhere in the back of her mind, and she will tell everyone she knows the same old story: her parents are on the Mainland for work or hunting polar bears up north, and they are staying with Aunt Deal for just a little longer. Just awhile longer, until things return to normal. Just a little longer, until Sheila finishes high school and Dennis and his wife can get their house built. Just a little longer, because Aunt Deal is so very weak these days, it's her heart, you know. Just a little longer, just until they can dispose of her effects, just until Dennis and his wife get settled on the Mainland. Just a little while.

The Scold's Bridle

There seems to be no remedy for the lashing, cutting power of a woman's tongue. A woman's tongue, some men believe, is the sharpest instrument on earth, capable of exacting great destruction, able to bring cities tumbling down, stop armies in their tracks. This is Martha's story, the story of a woman with a tongue so sharp she kept it hidden for fear of the damage it might do. She had been misled, as we so often are, into thinking that silence is a close cousin to acquiescence, that not saying what we think or want is virtuous and woman-like and proper. Martha is about to learn the error of this philosophy, as we all do, sooner or later.

Well, here is Martha, standing in the backyard of one of the finest houses in Guernsey, at least after the war, when nobody had anything, and those who had their own tiny portion took great care to hide it from the others. Martha was married before the war, to a Newfoundland boy from some other part of the island, down over the line, where nobody who had any sense lived. What was down there, anyway? Woods, the Exploits River jammed with logs, and further west, the Codroy

Valley and Port-aux-Basques, where at least you could escape to Nova Scotia if you were lucky. Pat was her husband, and Pat was from some place down around Corner Brook, some place where everyone eventually packed up and ran off, even before the sixties and Joey's plan of resettlement, before Confederation and all the other shiny dreams of government. When pressed, Pat would say he was from Corner Brook, which was true enough if you allowed him a span of some forty miles. His people were all dead, victims of some mysterious plague that had somehow spared everyone else. People in Guernsey didn't know much about Pat, and they didn't care, and when he married Martha just before the war, nobody thought much about it or spoke much, except to say it was the proper thing, for Martha was close to forty and not getting any younger. Nobody said anything, either, when Pat fell victim to the war in Europe and spilled his life out somewhere in Africa. Nobody cared, because he wasn't from Guernsey.

Martha's mother and father had been born in Guernsey and lived all their lives in the very house you can see in the picture. When her father fell off the roof one Easter Sunday and broke his back, her mother said the shock would kill them all, but Martha has managed to survive. Her parents lie side by side in the local cemetery now, their bones entwined like ivy branches, like the thickets of dense alders that line every road in Guernsey.

Years ago, when Martha was young, she spent a year or so in town, and took a secretarial course, learned how to answer phones and use the typewriter. This would be all right if she had stayed in town, but here there is little call for typewriting, or poncing about all day long in a tweedy business suit, and as for telephones, there's one party line for all of Guernsey, and those that use it say they're glad to have it. So Martha came back from town and set herself to work airing out the house after her parents died. This became so much of a thing that groups of children and old people would gather in the road outside her house, and watch as Martha tumbled sturdy wooden bookcases out the door, rolled her mother's washtub down the steps, and tore the fussy, lacy curtains from the windows. Across the way, on Belgium Road, Pansy Pike the postmistress could see everything that Martha did; Pansy told everyone who cared to listen that Martha was going to gut the house from top to bottom, and it wasn't decent, with her people hardly in the ground this twelvemonth. Who did Martha think she was? But still and all, it was great entertainment for all concerned to stand outside the old brown bungalow and watch as Martha flung away a lifetime's worth of cotton housedresses, her mother's tiny shoes, a box of rusty tools. She had no need of Perry Pike to come along with his pickup truck and haul the stuff away, for as soon as something came tumbling down the wooden stairs it was swiftly claimed and carried off, to reinstate its existence in some other house. In this way, Martha divested herself of everything musty and old — in short, nearly everything that was in the house. It was, she decided, long past time for a change.

She had used her time in town wisely, you see, and had learned far more than she would let on — learned about human nature and the wiles of the Devil, and the way to peace and resurrection. While paying out her year in town, Martha had come across a group of temperance workers, women of the Salvation Army, followers of General Booth, who preached against the evils of the demon rum. Martha understood that liquor was the bane and bottom cause of all that was rank and damaged in society, and it was her duty as a good Christian woman to eradicate its presence from the earth — or at least from Guernsey, which everyone agreed was quite possibly part of the earth, although no one was entirely sure. Martha wasn't precisely what you might call a good Christian woman, either, in that she nowhere embodied any of the saintly virtues. She had a great desire, however, to preach, or more precisely to rail, and this is what lay behind the sudden eviction of all her mother's worldly goods. She would make good use of the wide wooden steps of the house in Belgium Road, would outfit them as her pulpit and preach to the citizens of Guernsey on the evils of drink.

As with all seductive plans, there was a flaw: with the exception of some two or three older gentlemen (whose drink of choice was cheap aftershave or dubious home brew), no one in Guernsey really drank, as such. Ellis Tucker had been known to sneak a nip of home brew now and then, and once, at Daphne Barrett's shotgun wedding, old Uncle Jim had got into the rum, but that was the extent of it. Martha knew this, and she was unfazed by it. As far as Martha was concerned, she had a mission, and it was a sacred mission, and she was determined to fulfil it to the best of her ability. Thus it was that, on the very next Saturday night (the night most likely to give rise to drink-related evil and debauchery), Martha, dressed in her Sunday best, appeared on the steps of her house, clutching an empty rum bottle and a Bible. She stood there for some time before Pansy Pike, peering out the window with binoculars, espied her presence. Within moments, Pansy was on the Guernsey party line, informing all the neighbours. By eight o'clock, a group of small boys and giggling teenage girls had appeared on Belgium Road, and by eight fifteen, several old fishermen had made their way up from Harry Bishop's twine loft in the harbour, and were ranged about the front yard. None of them dared go past the front gate, however. As far as audiences go (especially for Guernsey), it was impressive, and Martha decided to launch right into her spiel against the evils of the demon rum.

"The *Devil* —"

This produced much giggling from the small boys.

"Satan, the *destroyer* —"

The fishermen shuffled their feet awkwardly. Jim Tulk pulled tobacco out of his teeth with a thumbnail, staring intently at the ground.

"Has caused your hearts to be hardened by *drink!*"

During this pause, Totty Rodgers unfortunately leaned out her kitchen window and began screaming for her children, desiring their immediate attendance at the family seat: *"Te-ed! Eileeeeeeeeeeeeeeeeeeeeeeeeeen!"* The group of people in front of Martha's house broke up, fractured into tittering groups and wandered away. Someone found a dead rat in the ditch and began a spirited game of football. Martha, still standing on the steps, visibly sagged. The hands clutching her Bible and her empty bottle of rum were anguished and regretful as she watched the hapless rat being gleefully bandied about. She thought about the evils of drink, the evil that was even now taking hold of Guernsey. She knew that she was powerless to stop it, powerless to stem the tide of sin. She had failed. Moreover, her misplaced desire for change had very neatly gutted her house of everything that she might need or could possibly use. It had all turned out so badly. It was like they said it would be, when she was in town.

Later, sitting in her denuded kitchen and drinking cold tea out of an empty jam jar, she heard the front door open — quietly, as though someone sought to sneak inside and do her harm. She laid down the jam jar, wrapped her hand around a heavy stick of firewood and crept into the porch. Here was Perry Pike, for once without his trusty pickup truck, decked out in his Sunday best and looking like a stick of chewing gum. Why had she not noticed before the way his dark Celtic eyes were fringed with thick black lashes? Why had she not seen the bulge and swell of muscle underneath the shiny blue serge coat? Perhaps her perspective had just now been altered, by dint of her experiences, and she could finally see what was in front of her. "I brung ye some apple jam me mudder made." He ventured forward, whipped off his cap, and set the jar on the sideboard. His hands, roughened by work and water, were tanned and brown, strong. Why had Martha never noticed? "And I wondered if ye might come out walkin' with me the night."

What would a woman like Martha say? This woman, the woman for whom the dark device of old scold's bridle surely was invented — what words might she frame to welcome this request? For he is a handsome man, and somewhat younger than herself, and might it not be worthy of her time in town if she were to reclaim the town of Guernsey from the wiles of the Devil, one man at a time?

"Come in and have a cup of tea," she says, and reaches to the cupboard to find another empty jam jar. She moves behind him, crossing to the porch, and closes the front door. There is a moment of regret because there are no curtains for the windows, and anyone can see inside the house. She won't let it bother her. Besides, her bedroom is hidden at the back end of the house, and it will soon be dark.

Darkness, she thinks, covers a multitude of sins.

How Phyllis Got Married

When Phyllis finally got married, it was a huge relief — most of all to her father who thought that he'd be saddled with her forever. Her mother, too, was relieved because Phyllis had been around the house for as long as anybody could remember and was beginning to get on her mother's nerves, more or less. Phyllis had that sort of effect on most people, actually, and there were very few newly-made friends who ever stayed around long enough to be considered permanent. Phyllis never *tried* to be uncongenial, but she had the personality of a neurotic. This could not be helped, no matter how hard anyone tried. Phyllis seemed to be afraid of the normal functioning world (this was why she had never sought employment outside her mother's house) and would not venture into it on pain of death. Coupled with this overweening terror of the unknown was the capacity to turn suddenly and snap the face off anyone, for any reason or for no reason at all. It never occurred to Phyllis's mother to enquire of the medical profession whether her daughter was perhaps a bit soft in the head — and anyway, as soon as someone managed to get her married off, she would be her husband's problem. Thank God. That responsibility would pass from her family to whomever this future husband might be, and Phyllis could, by turns, cling or snap, and all would be as well as expected.

Phyllis had no sisters and only one older brother, who had barred himself into his room six months ago because the electric clock on the Theatre Pharmacy was shooting secret messages into his brain. He had no immediate wants, however, that his mother did not meet: meals were laid upon a chair outside his room according to prescribed rituals, and a slop bucket into which he poured his body's waste was duly emptied into the downstairs toilet. All was well.

In point of fact, Phyllis's mother had been trying for years to pawn her daughter off. There were no lengths to which Mother was unprepared to go, and nothing apart from her objective mattered. She had solicited the attentions of longshoremen, sailors, members of the Benevolent Irish Society and an endless parade of American servicemen, all to no avail. As Phyllis neared her thirtieth year, her father began muttering veiled warnings about the convent and the Sisters of Mercy. He debated with himself whether Phyllis might be happier and better off in a life of Christian servitude. And maybe the nuns could educate her — send her to school somewhere, give her a useful trade of some kind. She could already sew tolerably well, and maybe she might repair the inevitable rips and snags in the other sisters' clothing. Anyone, he reasoned, could sew in black and white.

No one had any idea what Phyllis herself would like — no one had ever asked her and since she made herself somewhat useful around the house, there was no need to suppose that she wanted anything more. She has a rotating clutch of girlfriends, with whom she goes to movies or shopping at the majestic

Bowring's store downtown. It's impossible to tell these girls apart, and not one of them is in Phyllis's good graces long enough to be anything other than implicitly interchangeable. They are all rather like Phyllis herself: plump and somewhat dowdy, with bad teeth ill disguised by too much red lipstick, improbable hairstyles anchored by far too liberal sprayings of Adorn. In their company, Phyllis will behave abominably: taking off her gloves in public, laughing loudly with her mouth wide open, or gossiping shamefully. She will try on dozens of shoes at Parker and Monroe, shoes that she does not intend to buy. She will barrel past old ladies to get a good seat on the trolley, and then she will spread her parcels all around her, sit gawking at the window, cracking her gum relentlessly. A gleam will come into her eye, a gleam that is not exactly malicious, but intimates the possibility of malice. It is on one of these trolley rides that she meets Larry.

She is sitting as she always does, with bags and parcels strewn about. Since this is the week before Easter, she has also purchased a tulip in a pot, which she will keep in her room. It does not occur to her to purchase flowers for the family dining table, even though she weekly empties her father's wallet with or without his permission. On the day she meets Larry (a wet, blustery day in late March) the trolley is packed to the doors. Phyllis has watched the passage of several wet and hopeful people, but she has not moved her parcels, nor offered to give up her seat. Instead, at each of the trolley stops, she stares out the window at the lashing rain and smiles obliquely, as if all of it had nothing to do with her. Three old women totter unsteadily to the back of the car, treading gingerly on bunioned feet, and they stare at Phyllis balefully. "You think she'd get up and move," one of them says to the others. "Big girl like her." Phyllis feels their gaze burning into the back of her head, but she does not turn, and when the three old women get off at the next stop, a wild joy hammers itself into her throat. She has to press her handkerchief against her mouth to keep from laughing out loud.

She looks up to see a tall, thin man, with the rosy cheeks of a clown, standing over her. He is holding on to the seat with one hand, but in the other hand he carries what looks like a large suitcase. Phyllis eventually learns that it's an accordion. He likes the way Phyllis's entire body jiggles and shakes when she laughs, and he likes the bold and bloody scarlet of her lipstick. On Saturday night he invites her to come and hear him play at the Star of the Sea. Her parents have high hopes that this might turn out to be the means by which Phyllis is finally extracted from their house, and they view this promising development with the uncertain relief of someone who is to have a boil lanced. They hope the accordion-playing Larry will take Phyllis off their hands. They don't even mind if he presumes upon her virtue. An unexpected pregnancy — God forbid, and yes, it's a sin — would force Larry into matrimony. Phyllis's father is in a state of heightened anticipation all day long, and when she disappears out the door and into Larry's borrowed car, her father offers up a hasty novena.

The strange thing about their relationship is that Larry will never consent to see Phyllis anywhere except at dances when his band is playing. He never takes her out to eat, but he once allowed her a sip of his Coca-Cola when he went behind the Legion to have a smoke. Phyllis tries to normalize their relationship, but to no avail. She quizzes her cache of girlfriends, all of whom giggle and tell her to stop complaining.

"Sure, you got a fella, doncha?" This from Lillian, with sagging breasts and a bad habit of sucking her two front teeth, blackened by decay. "That's more than I got." Lillian is a telephone operator at the Hotel Newfoundland, and she has an Irish accent so thick that no one can understand a word she says. She is older than Phyllis, perhaps thirty-five, and undeniably homely. Phyllis realizes that she ought to feel sorry for Lillian, but she doesn't.

But what about Larry? How is she going to make him listen to her, let alone marry her — and lately her father has been publishing novenas at an astonishing rate. Phyllis, of course, has a modicum of native intelligence and understands if she is to effectively influence Larry in that direction, she had better strike right at the core of him. Nothing else will do. Next Saturday night, as Larry's band is packing up from a raucous dance at the B.I.S., Phyllis creeps behind the stage curtains and, concealed there in semidarkness, wrestles Larry's accordion into its case and spirits it outside to a car driven by Lillian's demented brother Dave. After Dave drives away Phyllis ventures back inside, fluffing up her hair and greeting Larry with an ingenuous smile. All night, Larry has been taking nips from a bottle of rum, and so there is a sort of grace period, when nothing is amiss, when all is in accord. Phyllis is sitting down to Sunday evening supper with her parents (her brother is barricaded in his room, taking apart an old telephone that he suspects helped the Germans to win the war) when Larry calls. Dave has told him everything. She must surrender the accordion immediately or Larry will not be responsible for his own actions. She is not given to understand what form this implied destruction will take — only that it will be swift and merciless. Phyllis takes the call in the front room, while her parents eavesdrop shamelessly. There is a period of silence as she merely listens. Larry is then silent as she explains her terms. He can find no other recourse. He must submit to her. He knows when he is beaten. As soon as Larry shows up with a ring, his accordion is returned to him, whole and intact.

On the day they are married, Phyllis's father gets so drunk on home brew that he can barely see, but he is happy: all of his novenas have come to this good purpose. No one besides Larry will ever know what Phyllis told him on the phone that Sunday night, the dark threats she made, the callous way she spoke of his accordion. If Larry knows what's good for him, he'll keep his mouth shut.

Danse Macabre

You never realize what a scruffy, barren and dry-looking place it is until you go back there in your mind, or until you see it in a photograph. When the details come into focus, when you can see every rock, every scrubby weed struggling for life, you understand — and you wonder how you could have ever found it beautiful. In this photograph, the hills look parched and burned, the yellow dust of the road seems to bake under the midday sun. Telephone poles stick out of the ground, probing at the yawning sky. The emptiness is hellish. This is a valley of dry bones.

Here are two men, skins burned to copper by the midday sun. They are sitting on the ground, feigning contentment, miming ease. The white-haired man has stringy muscles, probably honed in the coal mines, for he is from the north of England. He went into the pits when he was seven, leading a Shetland pony. When the seams were finally exhausted, a long time ago, the horses were accordingly sealed underground and left to die in darkness and in terror. This, they thought, was necessary, and anyway, the horses, once grown used to the abject darkness underground, could not reaccustom their eyes to sunlight. This was merciful. There is no place in this man's world for light-blinded horses. The white-haired man knows this, has embraced it as a tenet of existence.

The other man has come back from some far-off, foreign war. His sleeves are rolled up, and he is ready for anything. All day, while Angus has been here — the white-haired man's name is Angus, and he's the father of a girl that Steadman once thought of marrying — every day, while Angus has been here, Steadman pretends to work. He gets up early in the morning, even as the sun begins to blaze (this is Newfoundland; the sun isn't supposed to blaze, but it does) and unlocks the garage, rummaging with great enthusiasm among the assorted junk to find the old push mower which he completely disassembles in the middle of the yard, before carefully oiling each individual part. The garage is far too large and smells of dust and the desiccated bodies of blue bottle flies.

Once, Steadman found a wild bird trapped here, tangled in a spider's web. He caught it gently in his hands and held it, measuring the frantic beating of its tiny heart, and then he let it go. He thinks about the bird every time he's here. He wonders where it went, and he thinks he might like to see it again. Steadman feels that he has to impress Angus, and when he gets the mower put back together, he stalks up and down the shallow hills with it, mowing dust and weeds. He would really rather be sitting in the shade with a cold bottle of India Beer, but Angus is always watching him, and he can't afford to seem lazy. He attacks the weeds with a ferocity that surprises him, raising great clouds of grit. He wishes Angus had never invited himself for a visit, but ever since the war ended, Angus has kept in touch, and since Steadman was so often the recipient of Angus' hospitality — well, there you are. It's a debt of gratitude, that's what it is, and after all, Steadman almost married Angus's daughter Flora. As far as Steadman knows, Flora is still not married, but he has no intention of going back to Lancashire to marry her — it's been too long, and she is probably fat and blowsy now, her nasal Lancashire accent metamorphosed into an irritating twang. She would tell him how to run his life. She would come over here and immedi-ately gut the house, throwing out all his cherished collectibles: the Dutch beer bottles, the dried snake, the countless pairs of rubber boots in various stages of decay. Flora would want to manage him, and what good could possibly come of it? For the sake of an obligatory tumble in the wedding bed and an abiding conjugal coldness forever after, while she threw out all his stuff and cluttered up the bathroom with a bunch of useless women's things. No, it wouldn't do.

Flora was fine and good all those years ago, while the war was on. Angus liked it when Steadman showed up in his uniform to take Flora to the dances — that made him proud and gave him status in the neighbourhood. *See,* he could say to them, *my Flora's gone and caught herself a soldier.* And Steadman was quiet and polite, well spoken, respectful of Angus insofar as anyone had ever been. Angus was sorry when the war ended, and not only for Flora's sake. He likes it here, among the dust and rubble, far away from Lancashire coal and feeble-winded pit ponies, far away from Flora and her nagging.

He thinks he might stay for a while longer. Besides, he admires the way Steadman is so busy all the time. Angus never had a son. And Steadman, after all, is just like family.

He'll write to Flora first thing in the morning.

Sarah Two

Sarah and Beatrice are sisters — English sisters — living in England in an era when little girls' dresses were worn above the knee, and proper footwear was apparent. Eventually, some descendant of Sarah's will marry a Newfoundlander and find her way to these shores, but not yet. For now, Sarah is nine and Beatrice is five, and they are on holiday in Swansea, Wales. Beatrice enjoys going on holiday, even though in this picture she looks steadily at the camera, her gaze an accusation. Beatrice likes being on holiday, and especially in Swansea, for her Welsh grandmother sets the table every afternoon at four, and serves tea and sandwiches cut very thin, and fluffy little cakes with gobs of cream and lashings of jam. Beatrice also likes to wear her bathing costume all day long and get her bottom wetted by the sea, which is very wicked and naughty behaviour, as far as Sarah is concerned. Beatrice will grow up to be the evil daughter, the one the family holds up to ridicule, the one who will forever represent the family's favourite example of dissolution. In fifty years' time, Beatrice will be significant, chiefly because of her notoriety.

Sarah, too, is looking at the camera, but she's wearing the expression of sporting good cheer that always seems to be expected of her. Sarah is a good girl, the more reliable of the two, the sister who will likely spend her life and her heart's blood upon some undeserving man, spill herself in jagged bursts, until there's nothing left. And then she'll hear that he doesn't love her anymore, or that the has a mistress, and she'll end up alone, gazing out an upstairs window, rummaging through the scattered detritus of other people's lives.

Beatrice is wont to wander away by herself, and for this reason, Sarah has strict orders to keep her younger sister in view at all times. Sarah cannot enjoy her holiday, nor do any of the things that she might like to do, because Beatrice is sure to get into some trouble before nightfall. Sarah will need to rush to her aid, rescue her from the spines of various sea creatures, crab and kraken. She will need to spend long hours lying on the cliffs and watching the sea for mermaids, and if she so much as moves an inch, Beatrice will pinch her mercilessly, until tears come to Sarah's eyes. Sarah is patient with Beatrice, even when this virtue causes her pain. Secretly, she does not love Beatrice, but tolerates her for the sake of what she will in later years come to know as Duty.

But Sarah comes down with a nasty summer cold, as children will, and is subsequently barred up in her bedroom until the contagion has passed. Her grandmother has a very particular idea about illness and sprinkles white vinegar around the bedroom and out into the hallway, until Sarah feels choked with the fumes. Beatrice goes out onto the cliffs alone, escaping the clutch of her grandmother's admonition not to wander by herself. She is angry with Sarah for being ill, for not being able to conduct elaborate games with her. She wanders to the very edge of the cliffs and looks down at the sea, foaming round the rocks. She examines the clouds above her with a weather eye, the air of someone much beyond her years. She does not see the man until his shadow falls across the gently waving fronds of grass and sea plants. She remembers things her grandmother has told her, about talking to grown men she doesn't know, and especially after what happened to Sarah in the Tube station. It was talked about for ages by the adults in the house, especially when they thought Beatrice wasn't listening. *Left her alone for five minutes . . . went to look at the timetable . . . imagine.* Beatrice can't imagine: what happened, exactly? All she knows is that Sarah was ill for a long time afterwards and had to go to Scotland to stay with Mummy's sister Ivy and see a special doctor.

This man is the tallest man that Beatrice has ever seen.

"Where's your Sarah?" he asks. His ears stick out at an oblique angle to the sides of his head, and Beatrice imagines that he is able to fly when the winds are just right.

"Sarah's ill," Beatrice tells him. "She's caught a summer cold." She gazes out upon the shimmer-bright surface of the Atlantic, wonders what's over there, past the bulge at the horizon, the ocean's swelling flex.

"Where's your Sarah?" he asks it again, kneeling in the grass so that his eyes are on a level with hers. Beatrice thinks he must be a special kind of idiot to keep asking the same questions over and over. He has three hairs growing out of the top of his nose — three hairs that wave in the wind like antennae. He spreads his large hands in front of Beatrice: "I can do a magic trick."

He produces a coin, makes several passes with his hands. The coin obligingly disappears, but then falls out of his sleeve. Beatrice is unimpressed and turns to go. The shadows have become strange for her and the keening of the wind — the wind will, later in her life, always bring her back to this place, to the memory of it. Sarah can't go in the Tube station anymore with Mummy, because it frightens her, because something bad happened. Beatrice remembers the man and lady that came to visit Sarah at the house: the lady had black stockings on, and showed Beatrice her badge. They stayed a long time in the kitchen with Sarah and Mummy, drinking tea and talking. *Do you remember anything about his face, Sarah? Anything at all will help us.*

Beatrice sees the man again two days later, while Sarah is still being sprinkled with white vinegar and wrapped in boiled sheets. He hails her in the same fashion as before: his shadow, falling over the grass and falling over her. "Where's your Sarah?" and "I can do a magic trick."

"I've seen your magic trick!" Beatrice shouts at him, angry that he is interfering with her search for mermaids. "Your magic is rubbish."

He kneels so that he is on a level with her eyes. "Where's your Sarah?" he asks, smiling like a simpleton, the sea winds catching the flesh of his ears. "Did something bad happen to your Sarah?"

Beatrice kicks at him, infuriated. Far out on the sea, something flips an iridescent tail above the surface of the water, briefly, in the twinkling of an eye.

"Here's your Sarah," he says.

And there is Sarah, suspended in air, just beyond the man's outstretched arm. Sarah, wide-eyed and voiceless, sealed inside a bubble of clear sea water, her hair and her nightdress streaming with moisture, her skin curiously pale and sodden, the flesh of a drowned girl. "There's your Sarah, too."

The man and Sarah vanish in an instant, and Beatrice is alone upon the cliffs, in the bright Welsh sunshine, listening to the miraculous roaring of the sea.

Lacrymosa

Our Lady of Sorrows, pray for us. Here is a photo of the Byrne children, sometime in the early 1970s, when this island was still ruled by the Church, and family life was sacrosanct. So far there are only five Byrnes, but eventually there will be more, and if there are not any surviving Byrnes after these five, there will at least be attempts to make more Byrnes, for that is the way of things. To waste a sperm is a crime worthy of banishment to the deepest realms of Hell and Limbo.

Mrs. Byrne — Ruby — is somewhere in that nebulous wasteland between forty and old. The washing on the line — I can make out a pair of tights, a set of long underwear, and what looks to me like towels — is hung there by Ruby Byrne, winter or summer. She does the washing every day, with so many Byrnes in the house (and probably more to come). Here they are in the picture: Debby Byrne with her hands on Phonse's shoulders, and Phonse wearing what looks like part of a cricket outfit, but which is actually his school uniform. Their brother Wish is on the bicycle, the shine of it so bright in the September sun that it hurts the eyes, must surely dazzle anyone who sees it. Wish is proud of the bike, but the others will fight him for it later on. It isn't really Wish's bike; it is meant for all of them. This is how they will fight Wish for it: with teeth and elbows and the hard, knobby fists of children from a Catholic school. They will batter Wish nearly senseless, and when he finally relinquishes the bike, they will fight amongst themselves and argue over rides. Whatever comes into their family never lasts long: toys are battered into fragments, curtains and pictures are shredded, and books are abused in indescribable ways. Debby enjoys tormenting Phonse who whines obligingly; Ruby Byrne, up to her elbows in dirty dishwater, tries hard to ignore them, but her sink and countertop look out onto nothing much to capture her attention. She wishes her husband would come home, but she knows it's only noon, and the Brothers have given the children a half-holiday, which means that Debby, Wish and Phonse will fight amongst themselves and with the others, and there is nothing she can do to stop it. There is nothing Mrs. Byrne can do about anything. She knows not to bother, that there's nothing to be gained by trying, it's better to stay quiet, stay put. She isn't in the photograph — she isn't in any photographs, she's a barely visible presence, as evanescent as a cloud of vapour. But what about the other two Byrnes? Here's Rosary, standing next to Debby, with her hands on Paula's shoulders. Rosary is the holiest of all the Byrnes, and even though she has communicated this desire to no one — not even the priest — she is determined that the convent will be her destiny.

So here are the Byrnes, then, living in the centre of St. John's, and as far removed from life as if they were in an orphanage. Mrs. Byrne had no thought of this sort of life: she grew up on Empire Avenue with two younger sisters and counted herself lucky. On Friday nights, after Mass, she would walk down to Rawlin's Cross, down to Murphy's Store and perhaps buy a chocolate bar. This was in the Forties, during the War — there were lots of Yanks around in those days, Yanks in from Argentia, and Yanks living at Fort Pepperell, and oh my, they had such lovely teeth! All the Yanks had their own teeth, too, but Ruby Byrne — Ruby Trask, she was then — had all her teeth taken out when she was seventeen. "You might as well," her mother told her. Ruby's mother was massive, a great barrel of a woman with breasts like Gargantua and buttocks as large, round and hard as medicine balls. "Sure, they're only going to rot out of your head, then where will you be?" Ruby got into the habit of smiling with her mouth closed, even after she got her dentures. Rosary has her mother's bad teeth: small, wizened stumps, already rotting in her gums. It's a good thing that Rosary will never be married, Ruby thinks. Men would rather have a woman with a decent set of teeth in her head — a woman who isn't going to lose a tooth for every baby. Ruby wishes she had had good teeth, especially in the summer of 1944, when all those Yanks were around — lots of them, with their big, shiny teeth. On summer nights, Ruby and her best friend Shirley would go down to the dances — sometimes there were so many dances that the girls would recruit some daring friend with a motor car to drive them from one venue to the next. There were dances at the Benevolent Irish Society, and dances down to Fort Pepperell. There were dances at the Star of the Sea hall down on Henry Street. Best of all were the real fancy-dress dances at the Hotel, with all the Yanks in their uniforms, their shoes shiny and their hair nice. It was a real improvement, Shirley always said, to the kinds of dances you'd get at the Bella Vista or the Legion, with fellows like Harry Troke (who had the worst breath you ever smelled, and who chewed gum like a horse at the oats) or Dickie Brown (whose ears stuck straight out from the sides of his head like wings, and who wore goat rubbers underneath his good trousers). "I'd like to get the jesus out of here," Shirley always said. She usually talked like this as she checked her hair in her pocket mirror, made sure there was no lipstick on her teeth. Shirley had thick blonde hair and green eyes and a face that could be hard looking sometimes, but which was usually benign and open. "I got to get me a Yank," Shirley would say, "And get the jesus out of this place." And she'd snap her compact shut in the palm of her hand, with a noise like bones breaking. This always startled Ruby, made her jump. She wished Shirley wouldn't talk that way. She wished they could both get the jesus out of there. Every dance they go to, Shirley meets another Yank, each one the love of her life, until the next man comes along with a uniform and big, shiny teeth.

Shirley is in love every weekend, out of love again by Monday. Ruby wishes she had that kind of luck, but then the situation turns in Ruby's favour, and there is a smiling Yank in a fancy uniform and shiny teeth. His name is Roy, and he's here with his friend Donald. He's from Maryland, he tells her — some place called Hagersfield. The only place in Maryland that Ruby has ever heard tell of is Baltimore, where Poppy's artificial leg came from and where Jacky Pike's young fellow went, that time he got all burned up on Bonfire Night. Roy is a wonderful dancer, and he dances with Ruby all night long. Roy says that he and Donald are hoping to go to the Pacific and fight the Japs. "That's where the war is heading, yessirree." Roy walks Ruby home, negotiating the narrow streets of St. John's as though he were born there. It's very different from Hagersfield, he tells her, but he feels very much at home here. Ruby doesn't know what to do when he kisses her, and she shrinks from it, unwilling to let his eager tongue feel the sharp promontory of her false teeth. He kneads her breasts as though trying to extract some substance, milk or some elusive wine.

He tells Ruby a secret: he and Donald already have their orders and are being transferred to the Pacific as soon as possible. He tells her not to tell anybody, because he will get in trouble. Ruby listens to his footsteps disappearing into the moonlit summer night and wonders what will become of him, of all of them, and what will become of her. She imagines — although she does not have the language to frame it in this manner — that they exist in separate spheres, spheres that have touched and even intersected for a time. She wonders about Hagersfield, wonders if Roy will remember her when he's back home. She wonders if he might not come back for her. She hopes he will, but she doesn't think it likely. She can't possibly know the future. She doesn't know that Roy's body will wash ashore with Donald's on the beaches of Guam.

Kate and Cissie

Every summer for ten years, Kate and Cissie have come to Goat Island. As soon as school lets out in June, as soon as the last slates and pencil-boxes are put away, Cissie's grandfather packs the necessities into his boat, and they steam out of Guernsey's quiet harbour, heading for the open sea. Cissie loves to spend the summer holiday on Goat Island because she knows that Kate will be there, and in the glorious expanse of endless time between June and the first cool, yellow days of September, they will live in Paradise. Nobody lives on Goat Island anymore, but Cissie's grandfather owns land there, and his people are all buried there, and so Poppy calls it home. Likewise, Katie's parents have relations who fished for cod in the waters around the island for as long as anyone can remember, and so the other half of the island belongs to them.

Kate is to the left of this picture, and she and Cissie are seated on what looks to be a covered well, but which might even be some kind of root cellar, a means of storage. In this picture it is summertime, and Kate and Cissie are a pair of happy, sunlit twins. This is especially poignant because Cissie did not speak until she was four and rarely smiled or laughed. It is partly for Cissie's sake that her grandfather brings her to Goat Island every summer to see Katie. Katie and Goat Island make her happy.

No one is really sure why Cissie took so long to speak, although her grandfather knows that she has never been the same since the November gale that took her parents and took her grandmother. Her grandfather is all she has left, and he cares for her as tenderly as her own mother could. He is her entire world — he is everything to her. What could she know of a fine Saturday, a boat ride, a sudden vicious gale bearing down from the northeast? She was two when the tragedy occurred. She could not possibly understand the ways in which the sea can take, and take, and take again, until there is nothing left. She was asleep that night, safe at home with Bessie Tulk, sleeping safe at home in Guernsey. She was awake that Sunday morning when her grandfather and the men came back from the sea empty-handed. Her grandfather had been married to Tottie longer than anyone could remember. He tried to think about it, imagine what it meant that Tottie was drowned and dead, his daughter drowned and dead, and only Cissie left to take up the slack-jawed burden of his days. She is the only spark that remains to him. Every summer, he brings her back to the island. He needs to give her this small measure of indulgence. He needs also to give it to himself.

But all of this has very little to do with the story itself — this is background, details around the edges. Cissie is grown up now, and so is Kate, and Poppy has been dead for many years. In the end, he never sold the land he owned on Goat Island, but kept it in trust for Cissie, hoping that she would come back some day — hoping she would come back from Winnipeg, where she had found a job in a great big office building. But Cissie never did. She lives alone in Winnipeg, knowing no one, keeping no friendships, not even a cat. She prefers it that way. She is a secretary at a law firm, handling torts and civil cases, family law. She is neat and orderly, as tidy in her habits as a sparrow, small and curiously silent. She does what she is told; she has no secret life, nor does she want one. She has no aspirations or great dreams, no inclination towards art or dancing. What she wants most of all is to be left alone, for when she's alone there is a great, delicious void inside her skull, an absence like a noise that is not a noise, that does not make a sound. There are no thoughts in it, although it has the shape and colour of a November gale, darkly grey, ironic.

Cissie lives in a small efficiency apartment just the other side of Winnipeg. She goes up a set of skeletal wooden stairs that run up the outside of the building and enters directly into the kitchen, where she can lay her purse and packages down on the stove, directly to the right. To her left there is a curiously inclined narrow hallway leading to the bedroom, a bathroom the size of a broom closet. Cissie likes it here, chiefly because of its small size; it is finite, enclosing. She despises the lit sky-line of Winnipeg with a violence that surprises her, given that she so rarely feels strongly about anything at all. How has she has forgotten the smell of the sea?

There is mail for her today: the usual utility bills, advertising flyers, junk mail — and at the very bottom of the pile, a thin pink envelope, addressed to her in flowing script, a hand she does not recognize or know. The letter is postmarked from Guernsey. She reads it with a potent sense of apprehension, her limbs trembling. *You probably have heard that Katie is unwell.*

It's from Katie's mother, Marjorie. *We have been told not to hold out hope for her recovery.* And the final sentence, more poignant and more damning than the rest: *She's asking for you. Please come home.*

It isn't easy to secure a flight at such abrupt notice, but she does it. Before she realizes what she's done, the plane is moving east, and there is no escape. The self that Cissie has made, she leaves in Winnipeg, scattering what's left along her flight path, as if discarding shredded bits of paper. She knows that this should frighten her, but it doesn't. She is thirty-five years old. She is going home at last. When the airplane makes its final circle before touching once again to what she remembers as holy ground, she is weeping. She is weeping for something, she realizes, that is lost and gone forever. She can't unspool the warp and weft of time; she cannot unwind the clock and go back to her childhood.

Kate is waiting for her, sequestered in a private room. Cissie does not want to depend on chance, and so asks a duty nurse where Katie's room is. She cannot rely upon the vagaries of memory, a mental snapshot of two little girls sitting on a well. She needs more than this.

"Oh Cissie!" This is all that Kate can say. "Oh, Cissie." Her voice is thin and ghostly, shivering from the empty cavities of her shrunken body. The hands she reaches out are thin as well, as thin as bones, as hollow as reeds or flutes. Her eyes, enormous in her wasted face, are the colour of a November gale. Hers is a very particular pain, a pain as large as the world, but a pain full of words that sift and capsize, like blisters underneath the skin.

"I'm here, Katie." She wonders if she ought to say something more than this, something better, but she can't think of anything, and the sensation of holding on to Katie's fingers is similar to cupping a handful of cool rain.

"I wants to go home, Cissie." Katie's voice comes rushing towards her, like waves shattering on a beach. "I wants to go to Goat Island, like we used to do." (This will be her last and only chance.)

Cissie says the only thing that will make any difference: "When?" The lines and cables that bind Katie to the bed seem as large to her as anchor chains. "When do you want to go?"

It isn't hard to find a boat, a man to take them to the island. It is early May and the arctic ice packs have broken up, and the channel out of Guernsey Harbour is an unbroken swath of iridescent water. There is little conversation: Bert Hickey, whose boat it is, stands in the stern, one hand on the rudder and the other on his pipe. Cissie and Kate huddle on the narrow benches, luxuriating in the falling mist, as clean and soft as melted clouds. Cissie knows this is no ordinary crossing to the island. She knows it has some other quality to it, the taste of stone and tears.

Sing me a song of a lad who is gone
Say, could that lad be I?

Billow and breeze, Cissie thinks, mountains of rain and sun. All that crosses to this shadowed island, all that sleeps upon its shores is vanished and forgotten, lost like Avalon. They land in the mist; Bert Hickey pulls away. He will return at sunset.

Cissie hands Katie up onto the shore, astonished at the lack of weight, of substance. Katie will fade into the mist, disappear into the mossy hills.

They go along in silence, faces turned into the falling drizzle. Cissie is listening for something, some echo of long years ago. She leans into the mist, comes upon the old covered well and the little girls, side by side, giggling in white dresses, protected from the ravages of time. Their hands are cupped next to ears and mouths, and captured sunlight strikes fiery darts into their golden hair. Cissie sees herself and wonders at the existence of this fetch or double. A word from her, a gesture of recognition, and they will vanish. She wonders what specific realm they inhabit, where time has fled and left them un-scathed. She watches them in silence as the daylight fails. She watches earnestly, intently, examining the aspect of their faces, of their joy.

Bert Hickey comes at twilight with his boat and Cissie steps into it alone. She rides back to Guernsey wrapped in a blanket of the purest silence. *Over the sea,* she thinks, *Over the sea, goodbye.*

Harridan Shoes

Here is a picture of me. I think I must have turned my head at about the same time as Gerald took the picture, because my face is looking down, like demure ladies in old pictures. I particularly liked the shoes I had on that day — soft pink shoes they were, the kind of shoes a shrieking woman wears, a woman running for her life, or away from it. Hell hath no fury and all that. Harridan shoes.

You always think a certain thing when you hear that word, *harridan*. Like there's a film strip hidden away in the back of your mind, and when someone says the word, she springs to life: a shrieking woman with her hair all over her face, no lipstick on. *She'd claw the eyes out of your head, that one.* But in this picture I don't look particularly strange. I don't look scorned. Harridan is an old-fashioned word, with a richer pedigree than *bitch*. It's the word that women use when they're talking about some poor bugger's wife. He's always the one on whom the pity lands, not her. He's the one they feel sorry for. If he does anything to her, it's her fault, she drove him to it, with all her screeching and carrying on. You can hear the tutting noises, the knowing nods and glances: *went right cracked, she did, right off the head.*

I had a nice house, once, before all this happened. A lovely house, with a nice yellow kitchen and real wood floors. It's the little things you notice. Gerald was an accounts manager at Hussey's, out by the airport, and he made good money. Good enough, anyway. Hussey's was this huge store, all on one level, with clothes and stereos and chocolate bars and cat food. It was always crowded, and someone always on the intercom: *personnel from shoes to front checkouts for a price check, please.* They had bread machines and bikes and Christmas trees. Gerald took a course at the trade school, and when he finished he got a job at Hussey's, but that was fifteen years ago. He was always home at five-thirty on the dot, every night. And then this woman started calling the house, and he'd take the cordless phone and go upstairs. Sometimes, if I wanted something brought home from the store, I'd call his office and tell him to pick it up before he left, and I'd hear a woman in the background, laughing and carrying on. Gerald said, when I asked about it, that she was from the trade school, doing her work term out at Hussey's. "I heard her laughing in the background when I called." "She's good to get along with," Gerald said, and that was all. A hussy for Hussey's. All the other girls who worked there knew me by my first name and came over to the house at Christmas to have a couple of drinks and see the tree. Ina was the floor manager, a real big woman in her late fifties, with a huge backside and enormous pointy breasts stuffed into one of those 1950s bras. "Torpedo Tits" — that's what the young fellows called her behind her back. I suppose Ina weighed close to three hundred pounds. And then Gerald started going on these boat trips that Hussey's had for all the office staff once or twice a year, and Gerald and his new woman friend went in together on a dozen beer. He went down the basement and hauled out the old picnic cooler that we used to take in trouting with us and sent me up to the shop to get the bags of ice. The next Monday, he came home with a pair of shoes for me, the same pink shoes I have on in the picture, and said they were a little gift. I waited till he was in the bathroom, and I went through all the pockets of his coat, but there was nothing. What was I expecting? A scrap of paper with a phone number or a cocktail napkin with a lipstick kiss? There was never anything like that. And then one day in June he came home from the store and said to me, "I got something to tell you, and I don't know how you're going to feel about it." He knew exactly how I'd feel about it, and some part of him relished it.

I'd met her twice before that, once at a party we had and once when Gerald asked me to pick her up and drive the two of them to the bowling alley where he and his work buddies were meeting. I saw her coming out of the house, Darlene Sutcliffe, her name was. Sutcliffe, Slopwith, Slutwitch, Slaptits. She was married to some other guy, an alcoholic, and she had three grown youngsters, but her hips were tiny, like a girl's. I never had any children, and my hips are wide farm-woman hips. When she got into the car, she never said one word to me, except to point out where I needed to turn the vehicle. She acted like I was a taxi driver or a chauffeur. I thought about the things I'd like to do; I thought about driving the car into the ocean, and Darlene Sutcliffe still in it. *Boat trip, anyone?* When they went inside the bowling alley, I thought I saw

Gerald's arm slide around her waist. I imagined Darlene's tiny hips imploding in slow motion, crushing her internal organs and forcing her to the ground in agony. And then Gerald would forget all about her, develop a blessed amnesia, Darlene *who*?

When he asked me for a divorce, all the air went out of the room. I was stirring sugar into a cup of tea, there was a bird outside singing the same three notes over and over. My face was prickling.

I didn't even wait for the divorce to become final. One day while he was working at Hussey's, I took a pair of scissors and cut up all his underwear and socks and left them in his bureau drawer. I took every picture of him ever taken and cut the heads off, put the severed heads in an envelope and mailed them all to Darlene, care of Hussey's Department Store. I got some money from my grandmother and bought a ticket to the only other place I'd ever been. When Gerald and I first got married, we took a trip to Washington, D.C., and went to all the art galleries and saw the big stuffed elephant at the Smithsonian museum. Gerald took my picture in front of a magnolia tree, but I don't know where that picture is. Not all evidence survives. I remember running into Clarice Mutton five or six years ago in the mall; she had written a book of nursery rhymes, and that seemed a good thing for me to do. Clarice was always writing stories when we were in school, and drawing pictures. I can draw a little bit and do watercolours, and I knew a few nice stories that youngsters might like. I rented a house outside D.C., a white clapboard house with a fireplace and an upstairs, and I bought myself a drafting table from a nice black man and got everything ready.

And then I found a box of someone else's pictures and got interested in someone else's life.

I hear from Gerald now and then, and sometimes he sends a bit of money. Darlene finished her work term and went on a cruise to the Dominican Republic and met some Latin guy who liked her tiny hips. "Will you come home?" Gerald phoned one night and asked me this when I was drawing. It's coming around to summer, and the woman next door says it gets really hot here in the summertime. I don't know if I'd like it or not. She's from Ecuador, and she likes the heat just fine, but this house has no air conditioning. I might go back; I'm just not sure.

I threw away the shoes, you know.

Special thanks to my parents, whose help in procuring old family photos is hugely appreciated. Thanks also to Carol Hobbs, who scoured Boston-area antique shops for old photographs, many of which appear in this book. I am deeply grateful for the time and dedication of my editors, Laurel Boone and Sabine Campbell. I am also grateful to the City of St. John's 2001 Arts Jury.